The Cold Case
Paperback Copyright © 2021 Lorhainne Ekelund
Editor: Talia Leduc

ISBN-13: 978-1989698709

Give feedback on the book at:
lorhainneeckhart@hotmail.com

Twitter: @LEckhart
Facebook: AuthorLorhainneEckhart

Printed in the U.S.A

THE COLD CASE

Billy Jo McCabe Mystery

LORHAINNE ECKHART

The Billy Jo McCabe Mystery

Nothing As It Seems
Hiding in Plain Sight
The Cold Case
The Trap
Above the Law

The social worker and the cop, an unlikely couple drawn together on a small, secluded Pacific Northwest island where nothing is as it seems. Protecting the innocent comes at a cost, and what seems to be a sleepy, quiet town is anything but.

The Social Worker

Billy Jo McCabe wants only to help children overcome their troubled lives, as she herself struggles to forget the childhood nightmare she survived. She took sociology and prelaw at the insistence of her adoptive father, Chase McCabe, and learned how to use power tools from her adoptive mother, Rose. She loves reading in the backs of bookstores before tucking the book back on the shelf and slipping out without paying. She has a fondness for peanut butter and dill pickle sandwiches, has a three-legged cat named Harley, hates running (because that was all she did as a kid), and secretly binges on brownies and red wine on the sofa in front of her TV every Friday night.

She's never been married and has dated only twice. She visits Chase and Rose when summoned and shows up dutifully for every holiday with her family, but she has no siblings to speak of, and she feels a growing resentment for the mother who abandoned her in foster care. Despite proudly maintaining the same prickly attitude that nearly landed her behind bars as a kid, she has yet to speak up to Chase, who interferes in her life too frequently, ready to fix every problem, whether she wants him to or not.

One thing no one knows about Billy Jo is that she moved to Roche Harbor because it's the only clue she has about the last known whereabouts of the woman who abandoned her.

The Cop

Mark Friessen, son of Jed and Diana Friessen, has landed accidently in the role of small-town detective, a position in which he's going nowhere. Nearly married once, and broken-hearted three times, he's sworn he'll stay single forever, and he keeps his tattoo of a former girlfriend as a reminder that only fools fall in love. He's tall, attractive, and stubborn, and he refuses to live in the shadow of his two older brothers, Chris and Danny.

As Roche Harbor's youngest detective, he sleeps with a gun under his pillow. He has a stray dog that won't leave, and he swears that the only two food groups that exist are meat and potatoes. His favorite drink is black coffee in the morning, sugared coffee in the afternoon, and a shot of whiskey in his coffee at night to keep him warm.

****Each book in this series is a complete book, with no cliff-hangers, and can be read as a standalone. However, these books may contain references to situations from earlier books in the series. As with any long book series that focuses on specific characters, their changing relationships, and how their lives continue to unfold, you may find it more enjoyable to read the series in order of publishing, as there will be developments and changes in the relationship dynamics of the core characters.*

The Cold Case
A BILLY JO MCCABE MYSTERY

**What happens when you stumble across a case
that should never have been closed?**

**Detective Mark Friessen uncovers a disturbing
mystery: A little girl was taken, but when
evidence disappeared, the case was closed.**

While cleaning out closed cases, Mark discovers a file on
a missing toddler, Gabriele Martin. After reading the
two pages within, he realizes evidence is missing. The
only interviews, by the detective who previously had
Mark's job, were conducted with a bitter ex-wife and a
former business partner, both of whom pointed at the
father.

It appears to have been an open and shut case. The
father took Gabriele in retaliation for a bitter custody
dispute with her mother, and then he killed her.
Although no body was found, the father was charged
and convicted, and the case was closed.

However, an old woman the town has dubbed Crazy Carla disagrees. She says she saw everything, and she contradicts the investigating detective's notes, yet the local cops pursued only one lead, the father.

As Mark secretly delves into the closed case and realizes that nothing adds up, he reaches out to social worker Billy Jo McCabe. Did social services receive any suspicious reports about the girl or her parents? What Billy Jo soon discovers is a family of secrets, a volatile marriage, and a forbidden relationship—and the mystery of the missing girl, whose body has never been found, becomes a case that should never have been closed.

The feeling of being unprotected was one he knew well, a feeling no one should have to live with. Mark wondered when his instincts had become so deeply embedded, the warning that sent the hair on the back of his neck standing up whenever anything was off.

It was a feeling that just wouldn't fade.

Mark could never be vulnerable, and though he would never be willing to admit to his weaknesses, he didn't take kindly to the familiar sense of unease. After his fellow officers suddenly turned on him, everything he did had gone under a microscope, with problems coming at him in a way he couldn't have explained reasonably.

That had been a painful lesson that he was the only person he could count on.

Maybe it was why his lone-wolf mentality had become so deeply entrenched.

He took in Gail's empty desk, aware that it had been

a few days since he'd seen her, and listened to the chief on the phone in his office.

"What are you doing?" Carmen said, suddenly standing in front of his desk in her light brown deputy uniform, her dark hair pulled back as it always was.

She never smiled.

"I'm on phone duty," he replied, just staring at the phone on his desk, which hadn't rung in a while. He glanced back over to the chief in his office, who was leaning back in his chair. Whomever he was talking to, Mark didn't have a clue.

"So you're planning on just sitting there?" Carmen said, holding a stack of files. She could be quite direct.

"I'm doing as I'm told. Chief said watch the phones, so here I am." He gestured toward the chief's office, not missing the twist of her lips and something else in her eyes before she nodded.

Okay, maybe there was some humor buried deep there—at his expense.

"I'm sure he didn't mean for you to just sit there and stare into space. So come on, give me a hand. There is such a thing as multitasking. Pick up the portable phone and carry it with you. See how easy that is?" She didn't wait for him to follow.

Mark couldn't shake the feeling that the chief had been keeping an especially close eye on him as of late, putting him on what was beginning to feel like a very short leash.

"So what are you doing, anyway?" he asked, grabbing the portable phone and following her through the open door into the back, then down the stairs, old and creaky, to the basement, which was a place he didn't go often. The shelves there appeared dusty.

"Cleaning out files," she said. "We have to make room for cases. Some of these go back years."

Boxes were stacked high on the shelves, labeled with black ink handwriting on the front. Carmen had a box out on the floor now and was shoving the files she had held inside.

"What is all this?" He gestured toward her.

Carmen didn't look up from where she squatted. "All the case files. The current closed ones are in the first row. Gail is usually down here, moving the closed files. Those four sets over there are all the cases that were never solved."

He took in the shelves she gestured to, seeing the sheer number of boxes, and wondered whether he'd heard right. Why didn't he know this? "Are you saying more than half the files down here are unsolved?"

She stood up and slid the box back on the shelf. "I'd say a little more, but that's why you're helping me. Seems some of the cases are mixed up, some cold and unsolved in with the closed and solved. The chief also wants to make room by pulling out everything more than ten years old." The way Carmen talked was so matter of fact at times.

"Excuse me? Pulled out and put where?"

She lifted her gaze to him. Even though Carmen was hard to read, something about the way she'd said it had him pausing.

"Someplace to make room, as the chief said. Once a case is that old, the probability of it ever being solved reverts to just about zero. You know the stats. With us being an island with limited resources, all these old case files are just collecting dust." She tapped the box.

It had him looking at each one, and he felt that off

feeling again. Something had happened to someone in each of those files, and he had the sense that justice hadn't been served. "Are you talking about destroying the files? You realize you can't do that."

Carmen pulled a box out and shoved it at his chest, forcing him to take it. "You really do love to stir things up," she said, and he wasn't sure she was teasing.

He set the box down on a side table. "Carmen, laws are in place for exactly this reason…"

"Who said anything about destroying files? The chief just said they're to be moved out. We need the room. So go through the box, make sure everything is filed correctly and closed, and then mark the file with your initials to say you checked it. The year is marked on the box. Anything older than ten years is to be stacked by the stairs. The chief is having them picked up."

She didn't look his way. He realized Carmen seemed to understand the underbelly of this island better than anyone, how the law seemed to be implemented. She was rifling through a box, and he couldn't help but wonder what she was looking for.

"Picked up by who?" he said. "Or should I not ask? There are supposed to be procedures in place for safe-keeping—you know, evidence you don't want tampered with. You can't exactly have this getting out to the public."

She hesitated but didn't look up. Mark was suddenly more aware of the files he'd closed and tossed on a cabinet by Gail's desk. That was the first thing she had told him about how to handle a case file. She had always put the files away, and he'd never considered for a moment where they went after that.

Carmen didn't appear to be listening.

"You know," Mark said, "it's not lost on me that you won't elaborate on this. So tell me, are the files being moved to storage someplace? Where? For an island this size, there're a lot of unsolved cases going back years."

Carmen was now squatted down at the end of a row of shelves, and he could hear her rustling. Again, she didn't answer.

"Hey, what are you doing?" he said.

She appeared around the corner, holding another box, and he had to remind himself that she had never felt the need to fill any kind of uncomfortable silence. He thought she did it purposely.

"You really do talk too much sometimes," she said. "Here's a thought: Sometimes you may not want answers to the questions you ask. Just have a look through this one, too." She dumped another box beside him.

He took in the unlabeled front. Why did it seem Carmen knew something he didn't? He found himself looking over to her. He wasn't sure whether she hadn't heard his question or just didn't want to answer, but the latter seemed more and more likely.

He opened the box, hearing footsteps squeaking above his head on the floor upstairs in the old building. After taking in the thick files, he pulled one out that was thin, with not much to it, labeled *Martin*. There were only two pages inside, and he flipped them over and took in the file again. It had been closed, apparently an easy case.

"Carmen, this one is dated four years ago, and there're only a couple pages in here. It's a missing toddler, a kid…"

He was reading the report, by a Detective Singer, open and shut. His stomach knotted with a sick feeling at the knowledge that a little kid had been killed, but where were the crime scene photos? It seemed a lot of details were missing. His brow furrowed as he closed up the file and rummaged through the others.

He pulled out another thick one, listening to the silence. When he glanced up, Carmen was standing by the stairs, and he wasn't sure what to make of the way she was watching him. He gestured toward the thin file. "Were you here four years ago? You know about this case? Then there's this Detective Singer."

Carmen walked over to him and took in the file, looking over his arm.

"There has to be something missing, another file," he said, lifting each one out. He didn't know why this bothered him, sloppy filing, sloppy work.

"I doubt it," was all she said, flipping through the two sheets. When she closed the file, her expression was matter of fact again.

Mark pulled out yet another file from the box, seeing a different case on each one.

"Paperwork wasn't really the detective's forte," Carmen said. "He always seemed to keep everything up here." She tapped her head, and it took him a second to realize she was serious.

"Really? You're messing with me. That file has no crime scene photos. Where's the body, a confession, a few notes?" He took the file from Carmen, who seemed more than happy to let him have it. One page was labeled *Interview*, and a note at the top said *Open and shut*. "Come on. You have to give me something, here. Who was this Detective Singer, anyway?"

She shot him a heavy stare, and he wasn't sure what was behind it.

"Who is this? There's a note in here about a Crazy Carla." He took in the name underlined in red. "So are these the kinds of files we're packing up and moving out of here? This is sloppy. How many more are like this?" He found himself reaching for another file, seeing Detective Singer's name in there. Again, the paperwork was lacking, but all Carmen did was shrug. "I know you worked with him. Come on, Carmen, seriously, what is this?"

"Look, Detective Singer was here before me—long before me, if you get my drift. I was just lucky he didn't train me. The chief did. So go through the files there and have a look. Make sure nothing's missing."

He couldn't pull his gaze from her, even when the chief called from upstairs, "Mark!"

Carmen pulled in a breath and pressed her lips together, glancing back to the stairs.

"Downstairs," Mark called. He heard footsteps, and the chief appeared in the doorway, looking down.

"Have to make a run out," the chief said. "What are you doing down there?"

He realized Carmen had stepped away. He made himself take a step over to the stairs and looked up, still holding the file. "Giving Carmen a hand with all these old files," he said. He didn't know why he didn't bother elaborating.

The chief only nodded. "Fine, shouldn't take long. Just stack them and leave them. Gail's on her way in, and then you can get out there and make rounds," he said. Then he just stood there for a second, and Mark wondered what was on his mind. The chief just inclined his head and walked away.

Odd. He had been sure the chief was about to say something. He listened to the footsteps and the door closing. When he turned back, there was Carmen with an odd look on her face.

"You know, sometimes when a case has been mishandled, you can't say anything if it's not yours," she said, pulling her arms across her chest and nodding at the file he was still holding.

He wondered if that was a question. "Sure," he said. "That's one of the reasons I work out here. So what are you getting at?"

Her eyes were brown. She didn't look away. "That feeling you have when something isn't right… Not all cops have it. You know what I mean?"

He knew. It was that feeling he had, which seemed to always be there.

"Let me ask you this, Carmen. Did you hand me this box with this file because you know something was mishandled?"

She blinked and stepped back, then looked away just as he heard the door upstairs. "You know, why don't I do rounds for you?" she said. "Sometimes it feels as if the walls are closing in on me here."

There it was, her unwillingness to answer. Another complex woman who seemed to live and breathe secrets.

Chapter 2

Mark sat in his Jeep, the engine idling, taking in the white cargo van and storage unit.

Of the fifty storage lockers on the island, he knew only two were used legitimately for storing personal effects, one by a family man who couldn't part with anything, including the rusted-out '75 Gremlin that had been his first vehicle, stored under what he suspected were boxes and boxes of memorabilia anyone else would have thrown out, and the other an old-timer who was a hoarder and had been ordered to clean out the aisles of garbage that filled his house.

If anything, Mark had learned that storage lockers held the kinds of things people couldn't keep at home.

He was at a loss for words after realizing the Roche Harbor police department had a locker in which to store police case files, which should never have been handled by anyone who wasn't a cop. The van driver was yet another friend of the chief, Bill Burke, the son of someone who delivered goods on and off the island.

Burke didn't have the authority to handle the personal, private, and confidential case files the average person was never meant to have access to. Mark just sat there with his takeout coffee, counting the twenty-five boxes as the young driver stacked them one after the other into that storage locker.

Case files were never willingly turned over to the public, though he knew police departments and DAs loved to cite exemptions. Yet there he was, staring at a young man who had no link to the department, whom the chief had tasked with shoving boxes of old cases, closed and cold, into a locker anyone could access. Worse, no one else had any idea the chief had ordered this done.

He dragged his gaze over to the passenger seat and the file he hadn't bothered to tuck back into the box. Instead, he had sat at his desk, reading the two pages over and over while watching the young delivery guy carry boxes of files out the front door.

The only interviews regarding the missing toddler, Gabriele Martin, were conducted with a bitter ex-wife and a former business partner, both of whom pointed the finger at the father.

The body was never found.

The father was charged and convicted.

The case was closed.

He had to be missing something. Maybe there was more to the file, to this case. He was starting to think that Carmen may have led him right to the file. The woman knew more than she was letting on.

He heard the rattle of the storage locker door and looked back over to the chief's family friend, who padlocked the unit, climbed in the van, and pulled away. He wondered what any good defense lawyer would do with this kind of information.

Apparently, he still hadn't learned to look the other way.

Maybe that was why it seemed to him more and more every day that the line between the good and the bad guys wasn't as clear as he'd once believed.

He should go back to the station. What was he doing with this case, anyway? It was closed. The man was in jail. The contents of the file were likely lost.

That thought had him pulling out his phone, scrolling through his contacts, and dialing. He heard the ring, and then she answered.

"Billy Jo McCabe."

How long had it been since he'd talked to her?

"Hey, it's Mark. You have time for a coffee?" He could hear rustling in the background, maybe paper. She had to be at work still.

"Coffee? I've had enough for today," she said. There it was, the type of snarky response he thought they were past.

"Fine, then I'll have coffee and you can just listen. I want to ask you about a case."

"An open case? Who?"

He took in the file, wondering if she'd think he was crazy. "Not recent. Listen, are you at the office?"

"For another half hour."

"Then I'll be there in five," he said, then hung up before she could say anything else, tell him no, or avoid him just because she could.

He started his Jeep and pulled back out onto the

rural island road. Nothing was around, even just outside the downtown area, around the corner, and up a hill. Then he was pulling up in front of the agency and parking beside a brand-new Nissan Rogue. He knew it was Billy Jo's and wondered when she'd tell him that her dad had footed the bill for the car.

He knocked on the locked door and then spotted her in black slacks and a loose baggy brown cardigan. She flicked open the lock, and he took in her unsmiling face, the freckles, the blue eyes. Their awkwardness seemed to linger.

"You didn't say what case this was about on the phone," she said, so he held up the file, and she shifted her gaze to it, then back to him. She inclined her head. "Come on in."

He followed her back and heard another lady on the phone. Billy Jo gestured to a room with dim lights, a couple of chairs, and a navy sofa. He wondered if this was where families and kids sat.

"So what's the secrecy, and who is the case about?" She closed the door and pulled her cardigan in front of her as she sat down in the chair.

He knew the source of her unease now, all those layers she'd unwillingly pulled back, allowing him to see the deep scars she'd hidden from everyone, that vulnerability. But he'd seen it, and he knew she wished he hadn't.

He held the file out to her. She hesitated only a second before reaching for it and taking it. She opened it on her lap and flipped the two pages, and he could see her confusion.

"A toddler on the island, Gabriele Martin. Her parents went through a nasty divorce. Says there the father took her in the midst of a bitter custody dispute and killed her so the mother couldn't have her. The parents' names are Brice and Nia."

"And what are you looking for, exactly?" she cut in quite sharply. He could see her confusion when she looked up to him. "This is sad. A kid's dead, and the father is in jail, so what more do you need?"

"Can you just look in your system and see if a complaint was ever filed about them—maybe about the father, the mother, or anything about the baby? It's just a hunch I have."

"You're serious?" she said. He swore Billy Jo had mastered that heavy gaze better than anyone.

"Clearly. I can tell by your expression that you think this is a long shot, but come on, just humor me. Was a complaint filed? Anything in the system about this family?"

She hesitated only a second before turning in her chair and tapping the screen of her computer. "So tell me, Mark, what is it you're really looking for? What is this really about? There's a tragic ending to this story, but it has ended."

"Maybe," he said. She hadn't turned to face him, and he found it easier to talk to her back.

When she swung around, he didn't miss the alarm in her expression. Her eyes reached out to him. "What's really going on, Detective?"

He found himself shrugging. "Just doing my due diligence, is all. Humor me. Anything there?"

She shook her head. "No official reports or investigation under that name. So level with me. This is more than routine curiosity."

If he could level with anyone, he knew it would be

Billy Jo—maybe. "Look at the file, a closed case with two pages and very little information. Doesn't it seem odd to you that that's all there is to the case? A couple interviews, open and shut. A little toddler disappears, and the dad is arrested and charged in a matter of days, yet there's no body. How did she die? All that's in there is that the mother and a former business partner pointed the finger at the father, citing a custody dispute, saying the father had uttered threats that he'd rather see the kid dead than with the mother. No other suspects."

She was still giving him everything as he sat there on the sofa. There was a tap on the closed door, and she lifted her gaze when it opened and a dark-haired woman leaned in.

"What is it, Pam?" Billy Jo said. Even to him, she sounded rather short.

"Excuse me, but Grant called to let you know that the Turner kid is going to have to be moved again."

Billy Jo seemed so on edge. "I just placed him with the Lewises. What's the problem with where he is?"

Mark leaned his arm over the back of the sofa and took in the exchange between the women.

"Seems he has too many medical needs," Pam said. "They don't have time for a weekly trip to the mainland, and they said you didn't tell them about that. They said although he's a nice kid, they didn't sign up for this."

He thought Billy Jo swore. "That's such bullshit. The Lewises were well aware of his medical condition and his needs. Fine. Tell Grant I'll handle it."

Pam looked his way, then stepped out and pulled the door closed. Mark didn't say anything, because he could see her frustration by the way she touched her hand to the bridge of her nose before looking over at him.

"Tough case?" he said.

She shrugged. "Oh, just a part of the job I never expected to have to do, convincing foster parents to take a kid. It seems more and more sign up wanting the paycheck without being inconvenienced in any way. Like, he's a kid. Seriously, I wonder how any of these kids are ever supposed to turn out okay. You know, when I got into this business, I had that starry-eyed naivety, believing there were so many good people out there, looking to really make a difference, and I just needed to find them and…"

He wondered for a moment if that was really what this was about. "I take it you don't anymore."

She leveled her attitude his way. "No, long gone. Worse, it feels at times as if I'm selling my soul. There's always that something, like they only want a kid they can park in the corner and not have to deal with. Other than that…"

He was pretty sure that was pure sarcasm. For a moment, he considered what she had to deal with, and he didn't have a clue what to say.

She let out a sigh and then turned in her chair. "You know, Mark, it sounds like you're trying to open a case no one wants opened. The father was convicted, and he's in jail. Is it because of the lack of detail in the folder here? I can see it being an issue, but maybe it was lost or misplaced or destroyed. You said there was no body. Are you thinking there's more here?"

What was he supposed to say? Yes and no. Why was he feeling as if Billy Jo wanted him to leave it alone? "All I know is that file is incomplete, and the former detective, Singer, conducted what looks like an ineffectual, sloppy investigation. There's nothing open and shut about that case. Where's the body of this little girl? How did the father kill her? How the hell did any judge convict him based on this? I'm just not comfortable with the way this was suddenly closed. I guess I was hoping you had something in your system, like social services investigated a complaint, just something I could use to fill in all the holes I see here."

She was shaking her head, and he didn't think she was listening, just reading the file. Her brow furrowed, and she frowned. "There's a name underlined here, Carla Nevitt. I know her." She looked up and held the paper out to him.

He reached for it, seeing the note he'd seen on the last page. "You mean the notation calling her Crazy Carla."

She shrugged. "Carla has a way about her, but I'd say she's anything but crazy. If I were you, I'd talk to her. Maybe she knows something. People can be cruel sometimes with the labels they toss out." She closed up the file and held it out to him.

He wondered if her off expression was because of everything she was dealing with or if she was just tired.

"What exactly are you doing, Detective?" she said. "Are you thinking the girl isn't really dead? Is that what this is about? Are you looking for her, looking to stir something up? Because I have to tell you, I don't know anything about this case, and the last thing I want is more sleepless nights, knowing the kid has been abused for years or was dumped somewhere."

She just had to say the one thing he hadn't allowed himself to think about.

"I'm just trying to dot the Is and cross the Ts, find

out why a detective did such a sloppy job on this case. One thing I do know is when you're trying to find someone missing, it helps to know where that person started. So I'm starting with you, here. Family trouble is usually noticed by DCFS. You said there's nothing, so I'll talk to the mother, the business partner, and do all the due diligence my predecessor didn't. Maybe I'll fill this file with all the details a closed case should have." Mark made himself stand up, holding the file, looking down at Billy Jo, who didn't pull her gaze from him.

"Carla isn't crazy, Detective. Start with her. I haven't been here long, but I've had time to get to know the types of people here, the kinds who need services and see a side of the island no one else does. Carla is a good person, though maybe a little wacky and eccentric when she's off her meds. I shouldn't be telling you that, but if she knows something, if she saw something…don't automatically dismiss it."

He put his hand on the knob and pulled the door open, then looked back to the young woman he knew so well, who was more complicated than anyone he'd ever met. "Thanks," he said. "If you need a hand with anything, you know where I am."

She looked away and stood up, and he knew that was the end of anything personal. She wasn't going back to that vulnerable spot he'd seen her in. "If you run into any problem with Carla, let me know. I'd be happy to tag along."

He gave her a nod, then heard her pick up the phone as he strode out of the office. He tapped the file against his leg, and all he could do was wonder why the previous detective hadn't put any meaningful notes in the file to justify why a man had been convicted, why the case had been closed although no body had been found.

Yeah, sloppy was an understatement. Maybe he should take a closer look at this Detective Singer.

Chapter 3

"There are people on this island who don't talk to the police, no matter what they see," said Crazy Carla as she turned the burner off under the whistling kettle in her old yellow kitchen. Why had he pictured an old woman with curly gray hair and pop-bottle glasses, not the dark-skinned woman with shoulder-length wavy hair and big eyes staring back at him. She was plump in the middle, likely early forties, and was filling two mugs that already held teabags, mugs that had been resting on the counter when he showed up at the door.

Maybe she'd been expecting someone. Mark hated tea, but he didn't see anyone else there.

"Something could happen right there, right in front of them," Carla continued, "and they'd turn away and pretend it didn't and refuse to be involved because that's been drilled into them. Yet here you are after all these years, on my doorstep, after I made so many calls."

What the hell was he supposed to say to that reprimand? She was right, of course. And why hadn't Detective Singer made a record of her calls coming in?

"You know, I watch all kinds of crime shows," she said, "and one of the things they talk about when looking for a missing child is how critical the first twenty-four hours are. I assume that part's real."

He nodded. "Yeah, you're right about that. The first twenty-four are everything."

As the clocked ticked down, so did the chances of ever finding the kid, which was not something anyone wanted to hear. Again, why did it seem as if very few resources had been devoted to this case?

"Then I'm at a loss, Detective, as to why you're here now after so many years. Why didn't you return all my calls?"

"The detective you talked to worked here before I arrived, Detective Singer," he said. "It was before my time."

She frowned and waved her hand as she put the kettle back on the stove. "Before your time… I'll have you know I called that detective the minute I heard that little girl had gone missing. It was all over the island. She went to the daycare across the way." She nodded toward the window, then pulled a spoon from the drawer and jabbed it in that direction.

He could see a white doublewide across the way. He looked around at the old rundown singlewide Carla lived in. This was one of the only trailer parks on the island.

"There's a daycare here?" he said. He had left the file in his Jeep, but he could remember the notes, and there had been nothing in there about a daycare. He found himself looking over his shoulder, spotting his

Jeep through the door, parked right out front behind an old red Chevy.

"Mavis runs the only daycare here for the little ones. She has fifteen kids every day, babies to school age, and little Gabriele was one of them, dropped off that morning by her mother."

She lifted the teabags from the cups. "Come, Detective. Let's sit at the table with Jesus."

He paused, watching her walk the two steaming mugs over to the table. "Jesus…?" He found himself glancing up the hall, waiting for someone else to appear. When he turned back, she was watching him and gestured to an old kitchen chair.

"Yes, Detective. Will you join us, please?"

Again he hesitated, wondering what meds she was on.

"Why, I told that other detective I saw that baby girl over there," she said. "I was sitting here with Jesus, having tea like I do every day. I see everyone who's coming, going, walking by, driving in. I know the cars, the colors, the faces. I remember everything, and I told the detective that."

He strode over to the table, taking in the chair again. He wanted to look up the hallway, but he heard nothing. "Does anyone live here with you?" he said. *Like Jesus?* He hoped he was an actual person and not imaginary.

"No, Detective, just me." She was already sitting, holding the mug of steaming tea between two hands.

He took in the perfect view out the window, then the tea in front of him, wondering whether he was supposed to drink it or it really was for Jesus. He made himself look across the table at Carla. "So you're saying the day Gabriele disappeared, you saw her here at the daycare?"

"She was dropped off in the morning. I remember it well. It was only forty degrees out, and the baby didn't have a coat on."

Mark glanced back outside as an old Pontiac drove past. "That was four years ago, and you remember?"

"I remember everything, Detective."

"So you see the kids who are dropped off every day."

She tapped the table. "I see everything from here, Detective—just like I told the other detective when I called in. I know the vehicles, the kids, who drops them off and picks them up. There's the gray minivan that brings the twin boys, the white Subaru that brings the angel with the pigtails, but she's in school now…"

"So you saw Gabriele Martin being dropped off," he said, sensing she could've gone on and on. "Did you see her father pick her up?"

She put the steaming mug down in front of her without taking a sip. "Not that day, I didn't. I remember that day well. I was sitting here with Jesus, having tea, and I can tell you the father did not pick her up. It was a blue hatchback. I'd never seen it before."

He took in the woman and then dragged his gaze over to the door, realizing that the name Crazy Carla made sense. He wondered if it was the mention of Jesus that'd had the detective writing "Crazy Carla" and underlining it in red, dismissing everything she said and ignoring her calls. There was nothing in the file about a blue hatchback, a daycare, or anything.

"You sure about the car?" he said.

Carla stood to retrieve the sugar bowl, then set it in front of him with a spoon. He again wondered whether he was expected to do something with it, to add it to the tea. Or maybe this really was for Jesus and not him. Maybe he should let Billy Jo know the woman was off her meds or something. He pulled his hand over his face.

"I know my cars well, Detective," Carla said, "and the people coming and going around here. At one time, trouble found a way in here, but watching keeps it out. Now, why do you suppose that other detective never bothered to follow up with me?"

What was he supposed to say? Even for him, the jury was still out on her reliability. He took in the still steaming tea in front of him. "I wish I knew, Carla. Sorry, but I'm following up now. So you said it was a blue hatchback that picked her up, and it wasn't her father. Was it her mother?"

What was her name? Nia, and Brice was the father.

"It wasn't the mother, either. She drives one of those fancy silver cars, you know, with the star on the front."

"You mean a Mercedes?"

Carla jabbed a finger his way and reached for the steaming mug again. "A Mercedes, yes. I saw the mother drop that baby off only a time or two. Not exactly mother of the year. Always had that phone to her ear, talking and walking. Thought she was someone important, the way she didn't get off that phone as she handed her baby over. Never kissed the child goodbye or hugged her, not like the other folks who drop off their kids."

Yet it had been four years ago, he thought. "You're sure about the details, the day? That was a long time ago, and if you're watching every day, it'd be easy to get the days confused." Mark finally reached for the mug and the sugar bowl.

"Detective, that tea there is for Jesus," Carla said.

He lifted his gaze, taking in her dark eyes, and pulled his hand back.

"And I remember it well. She wore a red and white striped T-shirt and red pants, the same as on the local news. I listened to that mother cry about her lost baby, saw the father was arrested, heard they never found her, and here I sit, waiting every day for that detective to call me back, to come here. Now here you are instead so many years later."

He could feel the admonishment. At the same time, as he took in the tea, he knew her credibility was nonexistent. "Well, thanks for your time, Carla. I'll leave you to finish your tea." He gestured to the two mugs as he stood, knowing he'd be calling Billy Jo the minute he pulled out of there.

"So tell me, Detective, are you planning on talking with the driver?"

He wondered whether his confusion showed in his expression. "The driver? Which driver are we talking about?"

She let out a sigh as if she'd just told him. For a moment, something about the woman made him believe she was completely sane and lucid. The next moment, the feeling was gone. "I already told you, in the blue compact," she said. "The one who picked up that little girl, carried her out of there, and drove away. I had never seen that car, but you should know all this, because when I called the other detective, I told him."

Mark pulled in a breath and then lifted his gaze to the window again, seeing the white doublewide across the way. Why had Singer omitted all of this from the report? "Okay, Carla, let's start at the beginning again.

Tell me everything about this blue compact and the person who picked up the little girl," he said.

Then he'd track down this Detective Singer and have a talk with him about all the holes he was seeing in this case.

Chapter 4

Billy Jo had just closed the door of her brand-new Nissan Rogue when she looked over to her stairs and jumped. The detective was sitting there in the dark. She realized his Jeep was parked right at the side of the garage, and she hadn't even seen it. In fact, she couldn't even remember the drive home—all because the face of a little boy was haunting her.

Mark Friessen was about the last person she wanted to see after the day she'd had, pulling a kid from a home and knowing he blamed himself for once again being shuffled off.

"Detective, seriously, are you trying to give me a heart attack?"

He stood up and gestured to the stairs. "You should leave a light on."

Why was it that it sounded like a reprimand even though he was in her space, at her place? Awkwardness still lingered between them.

"Well, I didn't expect to be this late. So why are you

here?" she said as she pulled her keys out. She didn't miss the chuckle under his breath, as he seemed to find humor at her expense.

"Just dial it back a bit, would you? I wanted to talk to you about Carla. I think she may be off her meds. She sounded reasonable until she didn't. I was almost convinced she knew something about the case, had seen something…"

She waved him out of the way and stepped past him up the stairs, not willing to admit he was right about the light. She could hear him behind her, and all she could think of was the face of that little boy, waiting so quietly with his clothes in a garbage bag at the front door.

Her heart still ached at the knowledge that the moment would be yet another she'd never forget. He had climbed into her car without a word and was now in the home of the only family that would take an emergency kid. Was it ideal? Not really.

She shoved her key in the lock and opened the door, then flicked on the light and looked back to the detective, who she realized was not going away.

Damn, there was something about that red hair. He was attractive, alpha, though she wasn't sure she was in the mood for anything other than wine and silence tonight.

"I take it things didn't go well with that kid?" he said. Right, he'd been sitting in the office when the order came in.

"Nope. I mean, how do you tell a ten-year-old boy that he isn't wanted because of a medical condition that isn't his fault? Worse, he was waiting there for me. He apologized to me for being too much trouble, saying no one would want him. The hope that should've been in his eyes likely disappeared long before I met him. So no, things didn't go well."

She took in her cat, who lifted his head as Mark closed the door, and glanced at the sofa Mark had once spent the night on. It was too short even for her, yet he hadn't complained.

He stopped at the sofa and ran his hand over Harley, who stood on the arm. "I'd ask if you want to talk about it, but…"

Why in the hell did he have to be so damn nice at times? It was easier dealing with him as the arrogant cop.

She lifted the flat of her hand and shook her head. "No, no, and no, I do not. I want peace and a glass of wine to try to forget. Can I offer you one, Detective? I don't have any beer." She pulled open the cupboard and reached for a glass.

"No, I'm good." He waved off the glass, now leaning against the island.

She turned away and pulled open the fridge to reach for the bottle of red, chilled exactly the way she liked it. She poured it in a glass, then lifted it and took a swallow, tasting the chill and the subtle hint of blackberry. It was a welcome end to her shitty day. "So I take it you spoke with Carla?"

His blue eyes didn't look away at first. Then he shook his head. "Yeah, and everything was going well. With the attention to detail in what she saw, she would've made an amazing witness—that is, until she talked about her tea with Jesus. Doesn't exactly make her credible. I take it the meds are for…?"

She'd always liked Carla, but she could see the

detective was having a little trouble with her. "If Carla was off her meds, you'd know. Having tea with Jesus every day is her thing. It keeps her sane and functioning, and she keeps an eye on things in that trailer park."

By the way he raised his eyebrows, she could see he saw Carla how everyone did. She, though, saw the woman hidden beneath.

"You're serious," he said. He really was having trouble with this.

She was so damn tired. She lifted her glass of wine and set it down on the island. "Look, let me ask you how everything went with her until tea with Jesus came up. I bet she had an attention for detail that few do. Events, people… You were probably impressed, right? But I can tell by your face that you're discounting everything she said. Pity, Mark, because that's what everyone does, and she knows it, too. She hears the names people call her, as if she couldn't have feelings."

He took a step to the side, and she realized he was uncomfortable. "Look, Billy Jo, she won't be taken seriously. There's living in reality, and then there's fantasy. She's easily discredited. She made tea for Jesus. I seriously reached for the mug, thinking it was for me, being polite, even though I hate tea. She basically told me to keep my hands off. For a minute, I wondered if I was sitting in his chair, too. Who's to say she isn't delusional, seeing things that aren't there?"

She wasn't sure how to explain it to Mark. He was so far off base about Carla. How could she explain it to a man who'd grown up in the perfect family, who hadn't lived through the struggles that Carla had?

She ran a hand over her forehead and angled her neck to look over to Mark, seeing the unease there. He really was a good guy, but he would be a disaster for her. Then there was the coffeehouse girl she knew he messed around with.

"It's not that simple, Mark."

"It is for the law. Either you're a credible witness or you're not."

Right, that was just how the world worked. Everything had to be black and white and fit into only one box.

"I can assure you Carla isn't…" she started.

"Crazy? Is that what you were going to say?" he said. He really didn't get it.

"Look, Mark, I'm sure an argument could be made against me, too, if you want to cut right to it. Some people cope in ways that don't quite align with a normal, expected response. Although I'd love to tell you Carla's story, it isn't mine to tell. Just know she survived something that means her having tea with Jesus is a healthy way of dealing with something very few could."

She could see the way he was looking at her, which was beginning to feel too personal. She didn't want him asking more.

"What meds does she take and for what?" he said.

A much safer subject, but still too personal.

"She has a dissociative disorder. She takes a mix of anti-anxiety and anti-depressant meds now. She used to be on an anti-psychotic but hasn't been since her last episode. I know she didn't do well on one of the drugs, but I assure you she's taking her meds, a dose that works. She's functioning, and if she said she saw something, I'd believe her. Anything she saw, she's lived through something way worse, and she knows when something isn't right. She has her eye out, the kind of nosy neighbor who will speak up and not ignore something."

Mark narrowed his gaze, but she didn't think she'd get him to see Carla the way she did. "Yeah, you're talking about a personality disorder. I hate to tell you this, but that isn't a witness I can use. I can see why the previous detective didn't pursue anything. Any lead from her would be completely discredited. Mental illness is mental illness. She sounds great with her details, but that'll end when she's cross-examined on the stand and asked what time Jesus usually shows up for tea, what conversations she has with him, and what he says back to her. Crazy Carla. The first thing a good defense attorney will do is ask her why people call her that, shred her character. You vouching for her is fine, but the law doesn't work that way, and any evidence or leads from her would likely also be tossed out."

She didn't pull her gaze from Mark. She felt as if he always brought out the worst in her. "Excuse me, Mark, but it's not just that mental illness is mental illness. A personality disorder is a psychological response to something really bad that happens during someone's early years, a pivotal time for a kid. It can stem from emotional neglect, extreme trauma, or repetitive emotional or sexual abuse, or all of the above."

She knew Carla would never see justice done to her uncle, who was still married to her aunt. She still remembered how Carla had said so matter of factly that her family always had protected the men, and the girls were apparently all just very good liars.

At least she knew Carla had found a lot of peace in her teatime with Jesus. It made her happy, and convincing Mark of that wasn't something she was too interested in doing, not tonight, anyway.

"Hey, I get what you're saying, but you also know those types of personality disorders can have a person losing her grip on who she is and the world around her. Again, anything learned from Carla would be tossed out…"

"Excuse me, but we're talking about finding a little girl. I'm at a loss as to why every lead wasn't followed. Wasn't the only goal to find the missing toddler? I mean, who cares if the person who can lead you to her isn't credible? That's an issue for down the road, after she's found—or am I wrong?" she said. She could see how uncomfortable he still was about talking to Carla, how he still didn't get it. "Maybe I'm missing something about this case. It's closed, right? The father is in jail, convicted, if I remember reading from the file, so what else is there?"

He was looking at her cat, then over to the window. He shook his head before dragging his gaze back to her. "You ever have a feeling that something isn't right?"

Every day. But, again, that wasn't something she'd share. She only shrugged, not sure where this was going.

"Well, the moment I opened that file, took in the two pages, and read what was there, I knew something was wrong," he said. "Nothing in there tells me how they came up with the father. Ninety percent of all missing kids are taken by a parent, but there were no other suspects, and what I can't understand is that the body of that toddler was never found. Now you're telling me I'm supposed to take everything Carla says as sane and credible? If so, there's a very real chance the father is in jail for something he didn't do, because the detective before me ignored a key piece of evidence. Carla saw someone she'd never seen before, driving a blue hatchback. The person pulled up and picked up Gabriele from daycare. None of this is mentioned in the file, not the daycare, nothing. So what am I supposed to do with this?"

She stared at her wine, thinking of the little boy she needed to figure something out for, yet here was Mark, talking about a case she was glad she knew nothing about. Except now she did. "Well, I'd say you just answered your own question, Detective, or do you want me to say it?"

His vibrant blue eyes… She swore she'd have to be careful of him. He was the kind of man she knew she wanted to trust too much. He didn't say anything.

"If you're thinking about this and it's bothering you now, and you know something isn't right, will you be able to sleep at night if you put the file back and walk away without looking into anything? But as you said, the case has been closed, and if you pursue it and start investigating another cop's case, aren't you doing the thing that landed you out here to begin with?"

He pulled back, and she could see she'd struck a nerve. "You mean calling out a cop for screwing up, messing up, being sloppy?"

She only shrugged.

He swore under his breath. "You think I'm being stupid, walking into it again, because I won't look away?"

She could see how he was taking it. She rested her hand on the island and then slid her wine away. "No, I'm saying that if you're going to reopen something that seems wrong and sloppy on the surface, which could have you suddenly in the line of fire again, I would just make sure you have enough evidence before you show your hand. Talk to Carla again. If she gave you a lead, follow it. And when the chief tells you to shut it down and walk away, you may want to ask yourself how far you're willing to go to find the truth."

Chapter 5

"Hi, Detective," Billy Jo said. "Wondering if you could give me a call. It's about what we were talking about."

She hit end, after being sent right to his voicemail, unable to stop herself from stepping into things she shouldn't. She couldn't exactly leave the kind of personal dirt and details she had in a message for someone to overhear, and she wondered how long it would be until he called her back.

The only distraction from her miserable day had been the dirt she found on Mark's case. She slid her phone into her purse and then pulled her keys from her pocket, opening her mailbox at the post office in town. She pulled out the flyers and junk mail and closed it up.

"Billy Jo, hi."

She looked up to a man she hadn't expected to see again, and her heart thudded. "Jim. Hi…" She found herself looking back to the door, then taking him in. He was a handsome man, with dark hair, and the way he was looking at her wasn't as she would've expected. She didn't understand why the familiar ache settled in her throat again.

"How are you doing?" he said.

It took her a second before she realized he was really asking. Apparently, he had none of the hatred for her that she had expected to see. "Oh, you know, fine. Keeping busy with work and stuff. So how're the girls, Patty and Lisa?" *And how is my mother?*

He glanced over his shoulder as someone else walked into the post office. He stepped to the side, and she followed him, holding the junk mail in her hands. She pulled at her cardigan, holding it closed, unable to explain the irrational fear of someone having personal dirt on her, even if she wasn't responsible for it.

"They're good," he said. "Taking dancing lessons right now. Listen, I just wanted to say that I feel badly about how everything went down, what happened to you." He gestured toward her across the foot between them.

There was the pity. Man, she hated that. She wondered if that was why she could feel knots in her stomach now. She only nodded. The way he was looking at her, she wondered whether maybe it was time to look for a new place to work, another city, another home. Yeah, fresh starts were always good.

"Well, it is what it is, right?" She knew it came out quite sharply.

He didn't pull his gaze, nodding ever so slightly. "Not really. If you ever need anything, give me a call," he said. Then he reached over and touched her shoulder hesitantly. He turned and nodded to a postal worker behind the counter before walking out, and she could feel her face flush.

She took a second to pull it together before stepping out onto the street, where her Nissan was parked. Billy Jo had to remind herself that it was because her dad loved her that he'd overstepped again and bought her the brand-new wheels.

As far as Jim Jackson, she didn't want to think too long on that home front.

After lifting her hand in a wave to him as he backed out in his BMW, she took in the coffeehouse across the street, seeing the familiar black Jeep parked out front. She pulled open her passenger door and tossed in the junk mail, then gave it a shove closed.

When she crossed the street and stepped inside the mostly empty coffeehouse, the tall, rugged redhead was leaning against the front counter. The bell jingled on the door, and he looked over to her and stood straighter.

The tall, leggy blonde who ran the place reappeared with a takeout coffee and leaned over the counter for a quick kiss. Apparently, he was still with her.

Billy Jo hated that feeling of intruding.

"Come on, I'm closing up early," Sybil said. "You and me tonight. I'll make it worth your while."

She didn't miss the teasing in her tone, and she did everything she could to walk as slowly as possible and pretend not to hear what was going on between them.

"Billy Jo," was all Mark said instead of answering Sybil, who she realized was still waiting for him to toss her a crumb.

"Detective, I left you a message about that thing you were inquiring about," she said. She knew she sounded ridiculously secretive, and Sybil was listening to everything.

"Can I get you something?" Sybil asked her. She

could say no, but that would make this seem even more awkward.

"Yeah, how about one of your lemon teas?" She forced a smile to her lips, noting that Mark hadn't pulled his gaze from her.

"To stay or go?" Sybil said, ringing it in the register.

Billy Jo reached into her purse, pulled out her wallet, and tossed down a twenty. "You know what? Make it to go," she said. Sitting there would likely have her running into someone else she didn't want to see.

Sybil set her change on the counter before hurrying away to make her tea, likely so she could get back to her flirty personal time with Mark.

"So?" was all Mark said to her.

She realized he was still looking her way. "Last night, we were talking about that thing, you know…"

Sybil's back was to them as she poured hot water in a paper cup and tossed in a teabag, but the way she turned her head revealed that she could hear everything they were saying.

Billy Jo finally gestured to the small table over by the door, and Mark started toward it. She took a seat on one side, and he reluctantly pulled out the other chair.

"Is this where you tell me to drop it?" he said.

Okay, now he sounded a little defensive.

She shook her head. "No. I did some digging. Although I told you no complaint was filed, after I started looking into it more, I found something."

Sybil was making a beeline right for her with her to-go cup of tea that she didn't really want. "There you go," she said. "Sorry to keep you waiting." She leaned behind Mark and rested her hands on his shoulders, rubbing. It was a possessive move, the marking of her territory. "Do you have to get back to work?"

Billy Jo wondered whether that was her subtle way of telling her to go.

"Nope, done for the day," Billy Jo said. "Listen, why don't I leave you two to whatever it is you're doing. Mark, you can let me know when you want to talk about that thing."

She moved to stand, but he hadn't pulled his gaze from her. Instead, he reached back to find Sybil's hands still looped over his shoulders, as if she were draping herself over him. They were sleeping together, he was hers, and she wondered whether he had figured out yet that Sybil was reeling him in.

He pulled Sybil around beside him, holding her away. "Can you excuse us, Sybil?" he said. "Billy Jo and I have some things to discuss. I'll talk with you later."

Billy Jo reached for her to-go cup, seeing the moment Sybil got it. Then she shrugged and pasted a smile to her lips, touching his shoulder again.

"Yeah, for sure," she said. "I have some things to do in back. You two take your time."

She wondered whether Mark picked up on the slight, the way she rested her hand over his shoulder again before walking away, back behind the counter. She didn't have to look to know the woman wasn't taking her eyes off him.

"You care to elaborate on what you're talking about?" he said, actually looking around them, though the only other customer in there, an older guy, had just stood up and left.

"You wanted to know if something happened in the family," she said, keeping her voice low. When he only shook his head and gestured, she continued. "There was nothing filed about the kid. I checked her name and the father's, then read up on the case from different sites, but nothing went into any great detail about it, which I found odd. Then I remembered that although I haven't been here long, I work with someone who has."

She was thinking of Pam, who had run the local office for ten years now. She still didn't know why the woman had been so forthcoming that afternoon.

"I brought up the toddler's name to Pam," she continued, "said I had heard something about the case. She was an unexpected source of information. She said the couple's marriage was pretty volatile, and she knew the cops had been called in once before they were married. There's more, too. She said the family had secrets. There was cheating, you know, someone on the side."

Mark leaned forward and frowned, shaking his head. "So he had a girlfriend, did he? Cheating on his wife?"

She wondered why he went there, though that had been her first thought, as well. Billy Jo lifted the lid of her tea and shook her head. "Nope, the other way. The wife was cheating," she said, and she didn't think Mark could've looked more surprised.

"You're serious, really?"

"And you know what else?" she said. She lifted her gaze to Sybil, whom she could feel watching them.

Maybe Mark had some idea, as he glanced over his shoulder and then back to her. "Don't leave me hanging."

"That business partner, the one you said was the only other person the detective interviewed? According to Pam, he's the other guy."

Chapter 6

"You sure your girlfriend is okay with me tagging along with you?" Billy Jo said, sarcasm dripping from her tone, as she leaned over in the passenger side to pick up yesterday's takeout coffee cups and sandwich wrapper. She tossed them into the back.

"She's not my girlfriend," he said.

Sybil was…what? Just a girl he liked, a distraction. She'd been fun for a moment, but he was beginning to feel things going in a direction he'd never planned, and he realized they might not be on the same page. Maybe that was why Billy Jo's comment had him feeling an unease he hadn't felt in a long time.

"Well, I'm pretty sure Sybil didn't get the memo, because that girl is pretty taken with you," she said. "The way she was looking at you, she's got that possessive air girls get when the boyfriend–girlfriend thing happens."

He had to roll his shoulders, and he gripped the steering wheel a little harder, wanting the subject of Sybil to go away. He was starting to feel a warning that his casual playtime with Sybil could quickly go sideways. Sex was just that—until it wasn't. He knew it could morph into the kind of thing that ended in disaster.

No way did he have any intention of letting anything happen, because a relationship was something he didn't want.

"You know, Mark, girls think differently than guys," Billy Jo continued. "You gave her attention, had some fun with her, but you need to figure out what it is you want with her and make sure she understands. I mean, that tattoo of your former girlfriend that you keep on your arm as a reminder of your disastrous history with women is completely screwed up, and I'm the queen of screwed up. Just saying that what I saw today is a girl who's smitten with you, and far be it from me to point out the obvious, but it seems the feeling is mutual, because you're encouraging that. That's all I'm saying."

He dragged his gaze over to Billy Jo, glad he had his sunglasses on, wondering why she was pushing this Sybil thing the way she was. It wasn't her business what he did, who he saw, who he slept with.

"So now you're giving me dating advice. Is that what this is? And you're wrong about Sybil. She knows well where I stand, where we stand. Why don't we talk about you and who you're dating—or not? You think you get to talk about who I'm sleeping with, dissect my personal life, but you think I don't know how you prefer Friday nights alone with wine and brownies, just your cat and TV, no one else? I don't think I've seen you out with anyone, not since you've been here. Why don't we talk about that? Come on, there has to be someone you're interested in?"

Two could play this game. He didn't miss the way

she pulled her cardigan tighter around herself and looked out the passenger window. Considering how quiet she'd suddenly become, he'd just stepped into another no-go topic.

"I ran into Jim Jackson at the post office," she said.

He took in the island road, bordered by trees on both sides. For a second, he didn't know what to say, considering she'd just shifted the entire conversation right into danger territory. He knew well how raw the wound still was, and never in a million years did he believe she'd talk about this.

"When?" he said. "So how did that go?"

She shrugged. Right. When Billy Jo didn't want to talk, she didn't talk. He couldn't get over the difference between her and Sybil, who was never at a loss for words about anything.

"Just before I saw your Jeep at the coffeehouse," she said. "It was unexpected, awkward. What do you want me to say?"

"You brought it up, remember. I'm not the one who opened the door on the Jim and Carly conversation, but since you have, let's talk about it. I can see it still bothers you, but this is a small island, Billy Jo. You will run into them. I take it there was no invitation to come on over for dinner to get to know each other and mend fences."

The way she dragged her gaze over to him, he could see the anger, and he realized it was just a front for all her hurt. "I don't need a therapy session. He was kind, though, said to call him if I needed anything. It was weird, is all. So, about this case, how are you planning on handling the wife, the business partner? The former detective, from the sounds of it, did a shitty job with the case. So we talk to Mavis and Carla again, and what's the plan after that? I mean, my dad is probably one of the best lawyers out there, but as you said, this case is now closed, and a man is convicted in prison even though there are a ton of holes in the case. Did he kill her, did he not? Where's the body, and why did the detective interview only two people?"

She really did have a way of shutting things down when she didn't want to talk. He pulled into the trailer park, seeing cars pulling away and kids being picked up, and all he could think was to tread carefully.

"Well, you said it. The case is closed, but with a lot of holes. Won't know any more until I talk to Mavis. For all I know, Carla imagined the entire thing, and this is a waste of time," he said as he pulled up in front of the trailer that also served as a daycare.

He parked behind a white SUV and turned off the engine, then unfastened his seatbelt and dragged his gaze over to Billy Jo. She said nothing else, but she was looking around at everything and everyone. He stepped out of the Jeep, taking in the clouds that covered the sun as it dipped low in the sky, offering the muted light that was just part of living on the island. He pulled off his sunglasses and rested them on top of his head. He could smell the rain that was likely to start anytime.

He nodded to a man carrying a toddler, wearing a blue coat, and remembered what Carla had said about Gabriele not wearing a coat that morning. There was just so much to this case that he wondered whether he wouldn't have been better off never coming across it.

He took in the closed white door and glanced once to Billy Jo before knocking. Only a second passed before the door opened.

"Yes, can I help you?" said a short, plump older

woman with short light hair in an odd type of stiff wave. Her makeup was heavy, and her eyes were blue.

"Are you Mavis?" Mark said. He pulled his jean jacket back to show his badge, and her expression seemed a little alarmed for a moment.

"I am," she said. "Is there a problem?"

"I'm Detective Mark Friessen. I have just a couple questions I wanted to ask you. I understand you run a daycare here?"

She was nodding as she held the door open wider and gestured for him to come in. He motioned for Billy Jo to go first.

"Hi, Mavis," she said. "I'm Billy Jo McCabe, with DCFS." She held out her hand.

This time he did see alarm in Mavis's face. He stepped in and closed the door behind him, then took in a kitchen and a living room off to the right, which was filled with toys, shelves of toys.

"Oh my good Lord, is there a problem with one of the kids?" Mavis said. He quickly picked up on the hysteria in her voice.

"No, nothing like that," he said. "I'm actually here about a little girl by the name of Gabriele Martin. I understand you used to babysit her." He took in her frown and the knit of her brow.

"I assure you I have all my licenses," she said. "Gabriele? Why, that was so long ago. Isn't her father in jail for killing her? The sweet face of that dear little girl… The thought someone could do something like that to her is horrific. That kind of thing just doesn't happen here. And him! Never expected that of Brice. Shows how you never really know someone." The woman was thinking, remembering.

Crazy Carla didn't seem so crazy now. Billy Jo had her arms crossed and didn't pull her gaze from Mavis.

"Do you remember the last day she was here?" Mark said. "Can you tell me about the mother, the father? I understand the marriage was quite rocky."

"Well, I've seen a lot of problems in families, especially when there are young kids. The usual overtired parents, mostly moms, are dropping the kids off while mom and dad are fighting. But not little Gabby. It was always Brice who dropped her off. He loved that little girl. That was what bothered me most. I always figured I was good at reading people. Him, though… Apparently, he pulled off the best act, appearing to be a caring, loving father, so devoted to his daughter. The mother, Nia, now, she'd never win mother of the year. The only few times she dropped Gabby off, she carried her as if she were a damn bag of groceries. She handed her over with her phone stuck to her ear, not a warm bone in her body. Always the impression she was being put out. Like, how does a mother become that?" Mavis was shaking her head as she pulled her chubby arms across the middle of her blue and white striped shirt.

"Do you remember the day Gabriele disappeared, the day she went missing? I have a witness who says the mother dropped her off that morning, but someone different picked her up, not the mother or father."

Mavis dragged her questioning gaze between Billy Jo and him. "Well, of course, but what does that have to do with anything? I guess I don't understand why you're asking all these questions about little Gabby. The father is in jail, or is there something I'm missing?"

As she looked between him and Billy Jo, he could see her thinking, wondering. The fact was that she'd likely tell everyone he had been there, and then the chief would find out. He could hear him now in his head, saying, "What the hell are you doing, Mark?"

"There are just some holes in the case, is all," he said. "No body was ever found. I'm just doing my due diligence on an old file to make sure all the Is are dotted and Ts are crossed. Can you tell me what you told Detective Singer, who was handling the case?"

Again she dragged her gaze between Billy Jo and him, back and forth. He could see the confusion there. "Nothing," she said. "I never spoke with anyone. Now you're scaring me. Am I in trouble or something?"

"No, nothing like that," Mark said. "It just seems my predecessor didn't keep the best notes. It would really be helpful if you could remember who picked Gabriele up the last day she was here."

Mavis lifted her hand, walked over to a cabinet, and pulled it open. "I can do better than that. I keep notes, a record. It was three years ago…"

"Four and a half, actually. Fifth of May," Mark said. He glanced over to Billy Jo, who had been so quiet, but he knew she was taking everything in.

Mavis flipped through the pages of her binder. "Ah, here it is, right here. Well, this is interesting. Now I remember. I don't know how I forgot this. The mother, Nia, had called to say that she and Brice were getting divorced, and she was the custodial parent. He wasn't allowed to pick Gabby up or drop in to see her. She had a family friend pick her up that day, right here."

Her finger was pressed to the paper, and Billy Jo was already looking. Mark leaned over her, seeing the scribble and the name printed beside it.

"Dylan Parry picked her up," Mavis said.

Mark stepped back.

"Yeah, it was the first time I'd seen him, too, but he seemed to know the little girl," Mavis said. "Is there something I should be worried about, Detective?"

He only shook his head, then gestured to Billy Jo. "No, but because this is still a formal investigation, just tying up loose ends, I'll ask you not to talk about this. If there's anything else you can remember about that last day, or anything that could be helpful, give me a call." He pulled a card from his jean jacket and held it out to her. Billy Jo was already at the door, pulling it open.

"I will, Detective," Mavis said. "But I'm curious. Are you saying that Brice didn't kill her, that he's not responsible?"

Exactly the question he didn't want her asking.

"Didn't say that," he replied. "Just doing my due diligence, is all. Again, call me if you remember anything else."

He followed Billy Jo out the door, taking in the trailer court. Carla stood in the window right across the narrow road. She really did have a bird's eye view of everything. Billy Jo was already at his Jeep, but as he pulled the daycare door closed behind him, he stood still, hearing the sounds of the trailer park.

Carla was lit from behind as she stood in the window. She didn't look away from him but didn't wave, either. She looked odd, like a woman keeping vigil.

"Hey, Billy Jo…" he called out to her and gestured across the way to Carla.

Billy Jo lifted her hand in a wave, and Carla waved back. "Do you want to go and have a talk with her, say hi or something?" Billy Jo asked.

He found himself looking around at the cars, the

trailers. He saw no one else, and he shook his head, thinking of all the notes to be added to a file the chief had no idea he had.

"No, not yet," he said. "What I'd like to do is find out more about Nia Martin and Dylan Parry, who picked up the little girl. And more about the marriage that had come to an end. A bitter custody battle? I don't know about you, but I can't quite figure out why Detective Singer didn't bother talking to Mavis. Makes no sense. I've seen sloppy detective work before, but something about this entire case seems way off."

Billy Jo said nothing as she rested her hand on the door of his Jeep. There was something about her. He realized he trusted her more than anyone, and he didn't know when that had happened.

"So that means what, exactly?" she said.

"Do you have plans tonight?"

She frowned and shook her head. "Depends…" she replied. He didn't miss her hesitancy. He couldn't read her at all.

"Don't look so worried," he said.

By the expression on her face, he thought she might snarl. "I'm not worried. I just want to know why you're asking. Before I commit to anything, what is it, exactly?"

He reached for his keys. "Could use another pair of eyes. I think it's time I dug a little more into this case. Tonight. You up for it?"

She said nothing for a second, then nodded. "I guess I could be, Detective. So where do you want to start?"

He took in her casual, baggy cardigan. "The Martins, the business partner, and Detective Singer. I'm thinking tonight, we find out where everyone is today, track them down. Then we talk with each one of them, because as I see it, it seems no part of this trail was followed."

Then there was the chief. He still had to figure out at which point to talk to him and bring him into this. How had this case been closed under the chief's watch?

Chapter 7

She slid the pizza she couldn't finish onto Mark's plate sitting on his scratched and nicked coffee table. His dog, which he refused to name, was lying beside her on the sofa, whereas Mark was on his cell phone again. Who he was talking to, she didn't have a clue, considering he was about as forthcoming on everything as she was.

Even she was having some trouble with what Mavis had said about the family. She considered the notes Mark had scribbled in the file while they were eating, and she wondered how it was that this case was beginning to feel anything but closed. She wasn't a cop, but she knew that much. The system was something she knew well, and it still scared the hell out of her.

She glanced up, realizing Mark was no longer on the phone, and took in what was left of the large pepperoni pizza he'd picked up while they passed back through town. Her brand-new Nissan was still parked in front of the post office, where she'd left it.

"You care to fill me in on who you've been talking to?" she said.

He lifted his gaze, and his vibrant blue eyes seemed to carry a weight she recognized all too well. "Just finding out who's who in this long list of suspects," he said. "Nia Martin still lives here on the island in the house she and the mister owned. Brice is in jail, charged and convicted for life even with no body found, but I know which prison he's in. He owned a hot tub and pool business here on the island. Guess who his business partner is—or was?"

She wasn't sure whether she was supposed to answer. His mouth was tight as he slid off his jean jacket, and she could just see the edge of the blue ink of his tattoo from under his T-shirt. "I'm sure you're about to tell me, right?"

"The very same Dylan Parry who picked up Gabriele. The report in the file is from Nia, the ex-wife. She's bitter, calling Brice violent, dangerous, unstable. Apparently, one of the neighbors placed a call prior to this to report domestic violence. Brice and Nia were fighting, yelling. He pushed her, she slapped him, and Singer was the cop who attended the scene. He ordered him out of the house. I spoke with Carmen, and she filled me in. What I don't get is that there's no mention of that incident in the file. A week later, the girl went missing, and the rest is history. Brice was arrested, charged, and convicted. Dylan says he heard Brice say there was no way he'd ever let his ex have custody of his daughter, and he'd see to it that she never did. Apparently, he was furious with Nia and said it in retaliation. Believe it or not, the pool and spa business shut down and restarted under a brand-new name, right here on the island, and guess who Dylan's new partner is?"

Again, she didn't think he was waiting for her to answer. "I don't know. I guess maybe you should tell me."

He nodded, thinking. "The very same ex-wife, Nia. What I also just learned is that Nia and Dylan are living together right now…"

"So Pam was right. Wow, if they were messing around together before, that could've been the trigger to push Brice over the edge. You know men have snapped over lesser things," Billy Jo said. This whodunnit definitely topped a night of brownies, red wine, and Netflix.

"That's if he killed her," Mark said.

She didn't know how to reply. She sat there, considering, then said, "You think the little girl isn't dead?" That would be a twisted best outcome if a man was behind bars for a murder he hadn't committed.

"I don't know. Maybe I'm just reaching because I want a happy ending. I left a message for Detective Singer, though he apparently left the island and is working some nighttime security gig in Astoria. Would love to speak face to face with him and see his reaction when I ask him how he managed to close this case with the lack of evidence. He didn't follow any leads, and the trail wasn't really hidden. I barely had to dig. The more I look, what else am I going to find?"

She pulled in a breath. "It's still early, right? How about driving over to Nia Martin's and talking with her? I mean, since we're in it, how about questioning her again? You have her statement right here in this file, and if she's lying, the story will have changed. It's much harder to keep straight the details of a lie than the truth." Maybe she was more than a little curious to put all the names and faces together and see their reactions. It was starting to feel as if someone had planned for this outcome right from the beginning. "I mean, I'm looking at this file. Where is the confession from Brice?"

Mark just shook his head and reached for the file she handed to him.

"What about the DA, the judge?" she continued. "How could they even convict with this lack of evidence? It makes no sense—but at the same time, it does. I've seen things happen in the name of justice that people would never believe." She ran her hand over the dog's head as it looked up to her and rested on her lap.

"It's about a story, Billy Jo," he said. "I'd love to have a word with the DA on how he managed to convict based on just the wife and ex-partner. There has to be more, more evidence, more something. I just can't see a DA pushing this or a judge convicting it this easily."

She didn't know what to make of Mark's face. "You realize you need to tread carefully here."

He lifted his gaze from the file and closed it up again. "You mean before the chief shuts it down."

She knew she didn't have to add anything else. She continued to run her hand over the dog's head. The mangy mutt looked well cared for. "You said it, you know it. History has a way of repeating itself. You may be in the right, Mark, but I don't think I have to point out that opening up a case another cop closed can put a target on you, the kind that could end your career as a cop forever. I suppose security jobs at the mall are easy to come by, though," she said. She wasn't sure he appreciated her humor.

"Yeah, well, let the chips fall where they may. I've

already been warned about my tendencies to go all cowboy, but I'm not changing who I am. Ready?" He reached for his jean jacket and pulled it on.

"For what?"

He only glanced her way while he reached for his keys. It was dark out. "You said it: I'm now in it. Either I can drop you off back at your car in town or you can tag along while I have a talk with the ex-wife and the business partner and wait for a call back from Singer."

She gave the dog one more pat and stood, seeing the way he looked up to her. "No, I'll tag along. As you've pointed out to me, what else do I have to do? Since you've dragged me into this case, I'd like to see how it all pans out. She reached for her purse on the floor and strode over to the door, where she'd kicked off her shoes. He was still wearing the cowboy boots he never seemed to take off.

"Come on, dog, stay," he said as he closed the pizza box and put it with the plates by the sink on the counter.

She went to open the door, hearing the dog following her. "You know, Mark, you really should give the dog a name."

He followed her out the door and pulled it closed behind him, then locked it. The outside light was on, and she could just make out his Jeep. He flicked on a flashlight for her, shining the path toward the vehicle.

"He's not my dog…" he started as he stopped beside her.

"Yes, I know you've said that, but he lives with you and found you, so I'd say he's picked you. Give him a name."

It was hard to tell whether he smiled, as he said nothing. What he was thinking, she didn't have a clue.

"You should know I'm considering leaving the island," she said. She didn't know why she'd said it. She'd told no one else. Instead of waiting for him to say anything, she stepped off the deck and started walking the path to his Jeep.

"Is this because of Carly and Jim?" He was right behind her.

She reached for the handle of the passenger door and pulled it open, then shrugged. She couldn't shake the feeling that something was ending here. "Because of a lot of things. Sometimes you just have to know when you're done."

Before he could answer, and before her mouth could share one more thing she hadn't told anyone, she climbed into his Jeep and pulled the door closed. Once again, she felt that giant ache in her chest that seemed to never go away, but this time it was because of an arrogant redheaded cop she had realized she was beginning to lean on in a way she couldn't.

Chapter 8

The lights had been on when they arrived. The property was large, from what he'd been able to tell, and the woman who'd answered the door had dark hair and brown eyes, attractive in a way that had him taking a second look as they stood now under the high vaulted ceiling of the entryway.

"This is a nice house you have, Mrs. Martin," Mark said. He wasn't sure what Billy Jo was looking at as she strode over to the hall table, above which hung a huge ornate mirror. Everything about this house seemed so neat and polished. He knew when someone had money. It showed in everything.

"Nia, please. It's no longer Martin. I'm divorced. So I'm confused, Detective, on why you're here," Nia said, then dragged her gaze over to Billy Jo, whom he hadn't introduced.

He was still reeling over what she had said as they left her place. Leaving the island… He knew why, but he didn't know what to say about the situation with her mother, which he knew had gutted her. She was a spitfire, a woman he now realized was his go-to when something wasn't on the up and up.

"I'm just doing some follow-up on a file," he said, getting right to it. "It's about your daughter, Gabriele, and the day she disappeared. Can you tell me what happened and when Brice took her?"

The way her eyes widened, he thought she had stopped breathing for a moment. "Wh—what?" She pressed her hand to her chest and pulled in a breath. "Why would you show up here, asking about my baby? Brice is in jail. He killed her. End of story. Yet you show up here and drag up all those painful memories? This is cruel. What do you want? Is there a problem? I don't understand what this is…"

He heard footsteps coming from somewhere in the house, and then a man appeared. He had light hair and stood a few inches shorter than him, with a good build. The man worked out.

"What's going on here?" he said, striding right to Nia, who went into his arms.

"This detective is asking about Gabriele. I don't understand what's going on," she said. Hysterical and dramatic was an understatement, but then, she'd lost her daughter.

"I'm just following up," Mark said. "This is just standard procedure on cases to make sure all the information is there. It seems something may have been misplaced from the file, is all. I mean no disrespect, and I really want to extend my condolences for such a tragedy. I can't even imagine what you must be feeling. I'm hoping you'll be able to walk me back through that day and everything that transpired. At what time did Brice take Gabriele?" He dragged his gaze from Nia to the man with his arm around her. He didn't need to ask who he was, but he did anyway. "I'm sorry, who are you?"

Billy Jo hadn't pulled her gaze from the couple, and he wondered what kind of read she was getting on them.

"I'm Nia's husband, Dylan. I guess I don't understand what standard procedure has you here on our doorstep, asking about my wife's daughter. Her ex killed her, and he's in jail. You're opening up wounds that should be left to heal."

"I understand that. It's just that these cases are gone through routinely, and there seems to be some missing information. So who called the police? When did Brice take Gabriele? I understand Brice made threats to hurt her."

Nia didn't pull away from Dylan. She shook her head. "Brice wasn't living here. We were going through a divorce, and, like most, it was nasty. He was spiteful, and I was scared for my daughter, scared he would hurt her to get back at me…"

"I called the police for Nia when I got here," Dylan cut in. "She said Gabriele was gone, that he broke into the house, took her."

Nia was now nodding. "She was sleeping in her crib, and I went up there and she was gone. The curtains were fluttering in the open window, but I had left it shut. Brice even had a key to the house. I called Dylan, and he came right over. Brice was a spiteful man. I knew he'd kill Gabriele just so I couldn't have her. It's who he was, may he rot in hell."

An open window, and Gabriele had been in her crib, asleep. Yet none of that had been in the notes. He nodded, pulling out his notepad, and then scribbled down the details. "So he told you he was going to kill her? Or you?" He gestured with his pen to Nia, then Dylan. For a second, by the exchange between them, he didn't think they'd answer.

"Yeah, Brice told me he'd make sure Nia couldn't have her," Dylan said. "We all knew what he meant. I guess I still don't understand what this is about, Detective."

Nia looked over to Billy Jo. "So who are you, exactly?"

Billy Jo stood with her arms crossed. "I'm Billy Jo McCabe, with DCFS. This must be a terrible time. When did you realize your daughter was in danger, or could be, with Mr. Martin? I understand the authorities had been called in about a domestic dispute."

Nia pulled in a sharp breath, and he felt the minute this could slip sideways. The hesitation was there.

"You know, Detective," Dylan said, "I'm getting the distinct feeling there's something else going on here. The case is closed, and you showing up on our doorstep is bringing up painful memories that are best left buried. What's really going on here? Are you new to the island, Detective? And you have a social worker here, too. I'm not a stupid man. What's this really about?"

So he didn't want to answer.

"You're right that I haven't been here that long," Mark said, "but as they say, you need fresh eyes on a case. Although I'm sure Detective Singer had a way of doing things, due diligence means having everything in the file so that if ever Brice gets another shot at a hearing, the case won't be in question. We want to make sure there are no holes. That's all there is to this. I've seen it before, sentences being reversed and thrown out because the cops who took a report didn't leave the right notes in the file or didn't question things they should've."

Billy Jo was standing at his side, and he didn't have to look her way to know she had rolled her eyes at him and his quick thinking.

"Now, you're Dylan Parry," Mark said. "You were Brice's business partner, is that right?" He dragged his gaze between the couple, who looked at each other.

"That's right," Dylan said, nodding. "As I told Detective Singer, Brice could have a temper. He'd been furious with Nia. I'd seen it. He said he'd find a way to make sure Nia never got custody of Gabriele—that if she wasn't here, Nia couldn't have her."

"So he didn't say he would kill her? He didn't use those exact words?"

"Of course he did," Nia said. "We knew what he meant. During that fight outside, when the neighbors heard us, he said he would make sure I never got Gabriele, that I would never hold her alive again. He pushed me…"

"And you slapped him," Billy Jo cut in, her arms still crossed.

Nia's brow furrowed. "He said some really, really horrible things to me. He deserved it. He put his hands on me first, shoving me, hurting me. He'd have hurt Gabriele. I was protecting my daughter. You'd have slapped him, too, for what he said. He could be cruel with his words, and when he was angry, he was like a bull charging for a red blanket. There was nothing you could say to reason with him. He broke into the house and took her…"

"But you said he had a key, so he didn't break in," Mark said.

The way she shook her head, he could see she was rattled. "You're confusing me. Yes, he had a key, but he didn't live here anymore. Detective Singer told him he had to go and couldn't come back. He made him leave. Detective Singer knew he was dangerous, so he knew he took Gabriele and killed her. The detective knew it, I knew it, Dylan knew it…"

"But her body was never found," Mark said. "How did he kill her? What did he do to her?"

Nia's expression filled with an outrage he hadn't expected. "He only laughed. Laughed! What kind of sicko does that? He said we'd never find her, that she was gone." She leaned toward Dylan, who was rubbing her arm.

"So at the time Gabriele went missing, where was Brice staying?" Mark said. "I mean, you said the detective made him leave."

"He was staying with me, in my house," Dylan said.

Mark hadn't expected that.

Dylan shrugged before continuing. "It was a bad situation between Nia and Brice. I had no idea he'd do what he did, that he'd kill his daughter. When Nia called, I came right over."

"So Brice wasn't at your house when Nia called."

Dylan seemed to be thinking. Something about the couple seemed so off, rattled, maybe from talking about Gabriele—or maybe from something else entirely. "No, he was out. I had come home and he wasn't there."

"You worked together, were partners. Was he at work that day?"

Dylan seemed to grip Nia a little closer. "He was there."

"So did he leave work before you did, or was he still there when you picked up Gabriele from her daycare?"

There it was, something in his eyes. Would he deny it? Mark didn't have to look over to Billy Jo to know she was watching them intently, their reaction. He was still waiting for an answer.

"You know, Detective, if I didn't know any better, this would sound like more than doing due diligence," Dylan said. "It's beginning to sound as if you're reopening this case, and you're shining a spotlight on me, on Nia. So, if it's all the same to you, I'm going to decline to answer any more of your questions. Get out of my house."

"Okay," was all Mark said. That wasn't quite what he'd expected.

Dylan strode around him, pulled open the door, and held it wide. Billy Jo didn't need to be told, as she strode first out the door.

Mark took another second to look at Nia and how rattled she seemed. "Just remember something: Lying to a cop is actually a felony, and if you're hiding some-thing, I will find out," he said. Then he strode out the door. The outside light was now off.

"Detective, don't come back without a warrant," Dylan said. "If you want to talk to Nia or me again, you'll do it through my lawyer." Then he closed the door in Mark's face.

As he caught up to Billy Jo on their way back to his Jeep, she had her phone out and the flashlight on. "So what do you think?" he said. He'd never have asked anyone else.

They walked down the darkened driveway, past a fancy big white SUV and a blue hatchback parked off to the side.

"I'd say they're hiding something," she said. "But I think you already know that."

All Mark did was gesture to the car. He pulled out his own cell phone and took a photo. "Doesn't that look like a blue hatchback to you? The very same one Carla saw at the daycare, picking up Gabriele?"

She just stood there. "It does. So now what? You heard him. You can't talk to him anymore without a lawyer. All you have is a man who's already been convicted and is in jail for the murder. The case has been closed, and I'm pretty sure all of this isn't enough to reopen it."

She was smart—and right, he thought. "Maybe so," he said, "but at least now I have a trail I can follow."

Chapter 9

The dog was lapping up water in the kitchen. Mark knew it was close to midnight as he lay in the dark in bed, taking a minute to listen to the sounds of the night, the quiet. As he settled his thoughts, he slipped a hand under his pillow to touch the steel of the gun he slept with every night. Even when he closed his eyes, that feeling of someone coming after him never left. He never had been able to just look the other way.

There was something about Billy Jo. He realized she was at a crossroads, at her limit in terms of how much she could have the shit kicked out of her, emotionally.

The dog jumped on the bed and lay down beside him, and he ran his hand over the mangy mutt who'd shown up on his doorstep not long after he'd moved to the island.

"So you need a name. Guess you have no intention of leaving, do you?"

The dog rested its head on his arm with a sigh.

Then he thought he heard something. His heart thudded, and his stomach knotted as he stilled. He heard the wood creak on the deck, knowing someone was out there. The dog jumped down, and Mark tossed back the covers and reached for his gun, then slipped out of bed in just his underwear, barefoot on the cold floor. He didn't flick on the light as he moved out of the bedroom, hearing footsteps and then a knock on the front door.

"Who's there?" he called out, walking to the door, staying in the shadows.

"It's Sybil."

"Ah, fuck," he said under a breath he hadn't realized he was holding. His heart thumped. It was just that feeling from so long ago that had never left, the fear of retaliation. A bullet in the back of his head was something he'd expected in his hometown, not here. Yet after today, that feeling was again his unwelcome companion.

He flicked on the outside light and saw Sybil through the glass front door, her flirty smile. He pulled it open, and her happy gaze went right to the gun he was holding. Then she threw her arms around him.

"You weren't sleeping, were you?" she said.

He could smell the booze on her breath. He knew she'd left two messages for him already. He reached up and pulled her arm down, and she stumbled a bit. "Did you drive?" he said closing his door.

She giggled as she strode past him inside, her skinny jeans showing off her perfect curves. She dropped her purse to the ground and pulled off her tan leather jacket, and he stared for only a second at the open door before turning back to the problem staggering to his bedroom.

"I did. So what are you going to do about it, arrest me?" She turned around and held her wrists out to him as she backed into his bedroom, giggling. Then she lifted off her shirt and tossed it on the floor.

His dog was staring at him as if waiting for him to do something. He heard the squeak of his bed.

"Come on, Mark, get in here and fuck me right now," Sybil called out. She laughed again.

What Billy Jo had said earlier was like an icy splash of water, reminding him of how bad of a direction this was headed in.

"Sybil, what are you doing?" he said. He flicked on the light in his bedroom, seeing her lying back on his bed in just her bra and barely-there matching black lace underwear. Tension pulled across the back of his neck. Her shirt and jeans were on the floor, and with the look in her eyes, it would be so easy to just walk over there.

He looked down at the gun he was holding, the safety still on. He walked over to his dresser instead and rested the gun down beside his watch, then pulled open his drawer and reached for a pair of jeans. He stepped into them. He could hear her rustling on the bed.

"Mark, what are you doing? Come on over here."

When he turned around, she was on her side, looking over to him. Her lip was pulled between her teeth in a pout. At least now he felt closer to shutting this down.

"How come you didn't call me back?" she said. "I thought you wanted me. Come on…" She sat up, leaning forward. There wasn't a shy bone in her body.

Why was it that he could now see exactly what he hadn't seen before?

"You've been drinking," he said. "There isn't a chance this is happening, so no. I'll drive you home. Come on, get dressed." He reached down to pick up her shirt and jeans and tossed them to her on the bed, and he took in her instant frown.

She reached for his arm, grabbing it before he could step back. Her touch was so soft, and in her eyes he could see exactly what Billy Jo had said.

"Sybil, this isn't okay, just showing up. It's late."

"You don't want me? I thought there was something here with us, Mark, this thing here…"

"It was just sex, Sybil. You know that." He cut her off. The last thing he wanted was to debate the direction she was imagining this going. "I'm single, you're single, there's no commitment here. I thought I made it clear I'm not looking for anything, so let's just agree we had fun and leave it at that. I'll drive you home." He pulled his arm back, though for a moment he hadn't thought she'd let him.

He turned and walked back over to the dresser, where he pulled on a shirt and a pair of socks. Sybil was now pulling on her jeans, giving her back to him while zipping up her fly. She reached for her light brown knit sweater and pulled it on, lifting her long blond hair. She was no longer smiling. The dog waddled past Sybil and over to him, jumping on the bed as Sybil reached for the shoes she'd kicked off.

"You mind if I use your bathroom before we go?" she said.

He just gestured that way and watched as she strode off. He picked up the gun, tucked it in its holster, and fastened it to his jeans before shoving his feet into his cowboy boots. He reached for his jean jacket on the leather sofa as he listened to the water running in the bathroom.

How had Billy Jo seen something he hadn't? He

heard the door open and reached for his wallet and keys as well as Sybil's leather jacket, which was tossed on the floor. Sybil strode toward him, and all he did was hold it up.

"We should talk about this, Mark," she said. At first, she didn't turn around so he could help her with her coat, but then she sighed and finally did. She shoved her arms in and lifted her long silky hair.

Mark was careful not to let his hands linger. "Sybil, I'm not sure what there is to talk about, showing up here this late after you've been drinking." He just shook his head. Her smile, which he'd once loved, was long gone.

"You didn't call me back," she said.

There it was, that feeling something was about to go sideways. "We're not dating, Sybil. And I was working," he said. He'd never had any intention of calling her back.

"But you were with her."

It took him a second to understand what she was talking about. "Who?" he said, gesturing toward her, wondering where this was coming from.

"The social worker. You left with her, Mark. Everyone on the island knows you spend a lot of time with her. Is there something going on between you? Are you sleeping with her, too? I have a right to know."

There it was, the paranoia he was familiar with. "Okay, you're way off base. We're friends, we work together, and that isn't your business."

She stepped back, and he could feel the door closing on whatever this had been between them. "Are you friends, Mark? Because from where I'm standing and watching, you're interested, and I know she's interested in you."

"Again, it's not your business, Sybil," he said, cutting the discussion off before he had to deal with the jealousy that was beginning to rear its ugly head. "And just to be clear here, there was no exclusivity between us. I was clear, so I'm not sure how you missed that. You're the one who suggested sex, no strings. I'm not looking for a relationship with anyone. Now let's go."

He walked over to the door, and when she didn't move, he reached for her purse on the ground. He pulled open the door and nodded toward it. He could see how pissed she was as she strode past him, grabbing her purse, and walked across the deck. The outside light was still on and he could see the odd angle at which her car was parked.

"Sybil, if you get behind the wheel again when you're drinking, I will charge you and take your license from you," he said.

She stopped midstride but didn't turn around, and he could see that he'd said exactly what was needed to end this. Instead of answering, all she did was lift her middle finger over her shoulder and start walking toward his Jeep.

Chapter 10

Sybil's car had been gone by the time he'd climbed out of the shower. He'd thought he'd heard a car that morning and figured she was likely embarrassed after her escapades of the night before. He was still angry, too. The twenty minutes it had taken him to drive her home had been the first time Sybil had said not a word to him. After saying goodnight, he'd watched her walk into her townhouse at the edge of Roche Harbor.

This morning, as he pulled into the station, he noticed her car was parked outside the coffeehouse, which was a frequent stop for him during the day. The chief's truck was already there, and he stepped out of his Jeep and pulled his phone out, then thumbed over Billy Jo's contact info, remembering what Sybil had thought. She was way off base.

Billy Jo wasn't his type, and he knew she was considering leaving. He should call her, see if she was okay. He should also call that detective again, considering Singer still hadn't called him back. He could feel the fine line he was walking.

He strode into the station and hadn't even closed the door when the chief called out, "Mark, get in here!"

He glanced over to Carmen's empty desk, then tossed his keys on his own desk and spotted the empty coffeepot as he strode across the room, realizing someone was in the chief's office with him.

"This is Harry Singer," the chief said, "the detective who had the job before you." He gestured to an older man, round in the middle, wearing a light jacket over khakis. His hair was brushed back, and he didn't bother getting up from the chair he was sitting in. The chief walked around his desk and leaned over it, not sitting.

Mark stood where he was, realizing there was more coming.

"Harry, this is the young man who took over your job, Mark Friessen," the chief said, gesturing, before he pulled his arms across his chest. His face held the same expression he always seemed to have for Mark. "So, Mark, could you please enlighten us as to why Harry got a call from Dylan Parry last night, saying you and some woman showed up at his house with a line of questioning about Nia's little girl, Gabriele? Imagine my surprise this morning when I drove in here to find Harry wondering why you're suddenly running around, talking to people as if there's a problem with a case he closed. I told him no, Mark wouldn't do that. He knows you don't go around opening another cop's closed cases. So maybe you can fill me in on what the fuck you're up to now."

Okay, so this very well could be the end of his career as a cop. He could feel his badge tucked at his waistband and his service revolver holstered next to it. The chief could demand he turn them over at any time, and he wasn't ready for that. He didn't have what he needed to re-open the case, and he could feel the noose about to slip over his neck, ready to hang him.

"Well, I guess that's a problem," he started, "because I only stumbled across the file when cleaning out the cold cases. It was about a missing toddler, Gabriele Martin, and there were only two pages inside. That file should be thick with statements, evidence. After reading the two pages, even I knew evidence was missing, maybe shoved in another file, but I found nothing. What I can't figure out, Detective, is why the only interviews you conducted were with a bitter ex-wife and a former business partner, both of whom pointed the finger at Brice. Never seen an open and shut case quite like this. Your notes said the father took Gabriele in retaliation for a bitter custody dispute with her mother, and then he killed her. Although no body was found, the father was charged and convicted, and the case was closed. I can't figure out how. You even have a note in there about Crazy Carla—whom I spoke with, by the way. She basically pointed out the holes in this story. I mean, you never considered anyone else, and there's the fact that there was no body. How did the DA even prosecute this?"

He could see he wasn't winning here. In fact, the chief appeared ready to give him his walking papers. Singer made a rude noise and gestured vaguely toward him.

"Why did you never talk to the woman who runs the daycare?" Mark continued. "Did you know that Brice Martin's business partner, who gave one of those statements, picked up Gabriele that day? Did you know that

Nia and Dylan were having an affair at the time? You were apparently called out by a neighbor about a fight between Brice and Nia, and you sent him packing from his house, so where did he go but right over to Dylan's? Then the night Gabriele disappeared, Brice apparently had a key, but Nia said she went up and found the window open. There's nothing in the file. I mean, can you tell me, if he took her, how did he get in? Did he climb in the window and out with a toddler? I think not. That house has no trees anywhere near it. Did he walk through the front door? So what about the little girl? Where is she?"

The office door was still open, and the chief was now staring down at Singer, whose expression was pure asshole, as if Mark were the problem.

"Chief, come on," Singer said. "You remember this case. The father had made threats. We know it was him. In just about all cases of kids going missing, it's the parent. I stand by the case, and a judge convicted him. It's solid." He actually reached forward and knocked on the chief's wooden desk. "You know it, Chief. You remember the case the DA prosecuted."

"But he never confessed," Mark said.

"Of course not. The man was violent, a psychopath, a liar. Of course he wouldn't confess. There was enough there. Everything pointed to the father. A judge wouldn't have convicted him if it was shaky."

The chief still hadn't pulled his gaze from Singer.

"You know that's bullshit," Mark said. "I don't know how you managed to get a conviction based on that."

"Oh, you little shit, you know damn well this was open and shut," Singer said. "He's in jail. It's closed. Leave it alone if you know what's good for you. Chief, do you seriously hear this prick? Is this how you run the station now—a cop retires and you pick apart his cases? Or is there more? You know damn well I've put some real assholes away. It's closed. Are you trying to open a can of worms, get a spotlight shone on my cases so all those criminals walk free on some technicality? You know this can't happen." The man was spitting mad, and Mark sensed that he felt the station was the kind of old boys' club he'd never grown up in.

"Chief, if I'm questioning this, you can bet someone else will, too," Mark said. "This case may be closed, but how long until it's not? If another lawyer comes in to handle an appeal, the DA will question why you signed off on something so flimsy that even I'm seeing the holes in it. There are witnesses who were never officially interviewed."

"That crazy kook on the island has no credibility, and you know it," Singer said, addressing not Mark but the chief, who it seemed was now deciding the fate of a case that should never have been closed.

"Let me point out that the window to find Gabriele closed quickly because Detective Singer didn't look anywhere else. Where is her body? Where is she buried? Did anyone see Brice with the little girl other than a bitter ex-wife who was cheating on her husband with his business partner, who has every reason to point a finger his way?"

"Enough!" the chief shouted.

Mark could feel it approaching, the moment his wings would be clipped and he'd be told to shut it down, pack it up, and get out of there. But all the chief did as he stood there, his arms crossed, was lift his gaze over to

Mark. He seemed to be considering something, everything.

"Harry, give us a minute," was all the chief said.

The older detective hesitated only a second before walking out of the office.

The chief walked over to the door and closed it. His hand still on the knob, he stood close to Mark, staring at him with nothing friendly in his shrewd gaze. "You just can't help yourself, can you? You really stepped into it this time, Mark. I guess you haven't learned that you do not ever question another cop's case, especially when it's closed. I don't want this embarrassment on this island, in my department. I won't have it."

Here it was, the demand that he hand over his badge and gun. He'd be fired, and then the chief would likely see to it that he was on the next ferry off the island. But Mark didn't cower under anyone, and he didn't apologize when he hadn't done anything wrong.

"Chief, he screwed up, and your name's on it."

The chief made a face and then shook his head. The laugh that came out should have worried Mark. "No, you see, you screwed up. But now you're going to fix it—today. You go to Brice Martin. Get on the next ferry. I'll call the warden and let him know you're coming. You get him to confess and say where the body is. Don't care how you do it. You make it happen. Promise him anything, a deal, a shortened sentence. I don't care what it is. Then you're going to get your ass back here, and a press release will go out about how Brice had an attack of conscience and told you where the body is so the mother can have peace. The people here want as happy an ending as they can get, and you're going to give them closure so they can mourn."

He just stared at his boss, wondering what he expected him to do. "And if he doesn't know where the body is?"

The chief thumped Mark in the chest with his index finger, his gaze direct. The man was pissed. "I said you'll have a confession, because there's no way in hell I'm having some PR nightmare about an innocent man in jail. We don't do that. I don't do that. He stays there. The only thing you're doing is closing this case up neatly, the right way, without any more problems." Then he yanked open the door, fire in his eyes.

Mark could feel the dirt this case oozed with as he strode out of the office without a word, taking in the old detective, who was sitting at his desk. Mark reached for his keys, and all Harry Singer did was lift his hand in a wave as if he knew exactly what the chief had said to him.

"And, Mark," the chief called out to him.

Mark pulled the station door open and looked back as the chief strode out into the bull pen.

"You're out of chances," the chief said. "No more of this cowboy bullshit."

He didn't nod. He said nothing as he walked out the door, pulled it behind him, and wondered what the hell he was going to do now.

Chapter 11

Her cell phone dinged just as she hung up the office phone, trying to figure out what to do with a little boy who was quickly slipping through the cracks to be forever lost. Yet again, she hadn't found one family who would actually do right by him. She thought of his mother, then of her boss, who still hadn't replied to her request to broaden the search.

There were days she wanted go back home, crawl into bed, and pull the covers over her head. She wondered now if this was why she'd been forced to live in the places she had, with the kinds of people who should never have been allowed to care for a kid.

She reached for her phone, seeing a text from Mark.

Have to go off island, prison visit. You want to tag along?

She took in the cubicle she was sitting in, her closed laptop, then looked down to the phone again and texted back to him, *Sure, when?*

Three dots signaled that he was texting back. *Now! Pulling up in front of your office. We're catching the next ferry.*

She glanced at the time and knew the ferry would be

pulling in any minute. She grabbed her bag, shoved in her laptop, and pulled her sweater from where she'd tossed it over her chair, then called out, "Pam, I'm out of the office for the rest of the day. I have my cell phone with me. Call if anything comes up."

She didn't wait for her to answer as she hurried to the door, feeling for a second that she was playing hooky when she should've been beating her head against the wall. It was a horrible feeling. Maybe getting off the island for a moment would help her come back with a different perspective.

She had her keys out, and she unlocked the door and stepped out, seeing Mark in his idling Jeep. She shoved the key in the lock and locked it behind her.

She pulled open the passenger door to see Mark in sunglasses and his jean jacket.

"Come on, hurry up," he said. "I want to be on this ferry."

She'd just closed the door when he put the Jeep in gear and pulled away. She reached for the seat belt as he pulled out of the parking lot toward the ferry traffic, where cars were already lined up.

"So you really are pursuing this," she said, noting his lack of a greeting. But then, Mark wasn't known for being chatty. "Take it Brice Martin is who we're seeing. You hear back from the detective?"

He pulled up and stopped at the end of the line, idling the Jeep. The ferry was now in and unloading, and she looked at the cars ahead and wondered whether they'd get on.

"Imagine my surprise this morning when I walked in, and who was sitting in the chief's office but the retired detective?" He only glanced her way, and even though he had sunglasses on, she could see the pissed-off expression he didn't even try to hide. "You know, Singer," he added.

She wondered whether her mouth gaped, because even she hadn't seen that one coming. "Wait, what? And the chief was there?"

He only nodded as the line of cars started moving. The ferry was loading. Then he shook his head, and she didn't have to ask how badly it went. She could see he'd taken the brunt of something.

"Chief knows everything now. Seems good old Detective Singer received a call from Nia and Dylan, likely right after we left last night, which has me wondering a lot of things, namely what's going on between them and the detective. Why would they have contact with him? He doesn't even live here anymore. Worse is that he figured the way to handle it was to drive here and shut me down. Had to have been on the first ferry over this morning. Was in the chief's office, and he left me with no alternative but to show my hand before I was ready. Not even a phone call from the detective, which tells me he's hiding something."

They were the last vehicle to fit on the ferry, and as Mark turned off the Jeep, she just stared at him, knowing she should say something. Finally, she said, "You still have a job?"

She thought his groan was a laugh as he leaned his head back against the seat. "Not sure for how long, but this trip to the prison was ordered by the chief. With the lack of information, it became clear this morning that the chief is interested in seeing this wrapped up nice and tight. The notes weren't there before, but I guarantee there won't be any question left in the file now. Worse, I expect he may even put a spin on it. The prison trip is to see Brice, but the chief expects a confession, for him to tell me where his daughter's body is. He basically ordered me to get it any way I can, offer anything. But whatever I offer, I promise he'll never get it."

She was trying to wrap her head around what he was saying. "Does the chief know Detective Singer screwed the case up?"

Mark rested his sunglasses on top of his head. She could see his eyes now, which had the knot twisting in her stomach even tighter. "Oh, it's an absolute shitshow, I guarantee that much. You think the chief doesn't know exactly what's going on under him? As he told me at one time, he knows everything that goes on on his island. The fact that Singer worked as long as he did says something. Worse, the chief knows he screwed up, but instead of wanting to fix it, he's worried about the PR nightmare of a possible innocent man in jail. He made it clear to me that isn't going to be a possibility."

She didn't even know how to respond, and maybe Mark had an idea that she was having trouble understanding. "So I have a question," she said. "What's expected if he won't confess to the crime and tell you where the body is? Let me toss this out to you in case you haven't thought about it: What if he didn't do it? You mentioned the chief doesn't want the PR nightmare of an innocent man behind bars, so what exactly does that mean? Is he expecting you to see to it that Brice confesses to something he didn't do?"

Mark was now looking straight ahead, out the windshield, and she could feel the ferry moving. He didn't say anything for a second, then slid his gaze back over to her. The blue of his eyes, the way he was looking at her, made her want to reach for her sweater at her feet and shrug it on. She didn't know why she was beginning to feel so damn uncomfortable around him.

"I think you already know the answer to that," he said.

She pulled her tongue over her teeth. "And you'd just do it?" She reached for the shoulder strap of her seatbelt, which was resting over her white T-shirt.

"I hope you know me better than that," he replied. He was looking at her again, and then he dragged his gaze down, taking all of her in before looking away. There was something about him today that had her more uneasy around him than usual. He didn't look her way when he said, "You were right about Sybil."

All she could do was stare at him before pulling her own gaze and looking straight ahead, seeing the cars on the deck and the open ocean ahead of them. If she looked back, she could see the island behind them. "About?" she finally said.

This time, she thought his lips hinted at a rather sad smile. "She wanted more, expected more. How the hell did I misread that?"

What was she supposed to say to the man she'd always considered arrogant, too good looking, who'd stood beside her at her lowest point? "You're a guy, she's a girl. You think differently. Someone wrote a book about it."

This time, he laughed, and even she couldn't help smiling. "Oh, Billy Jo, not sure what I'd do on this island if you left. You're not still thinking about it, are you?"

In fact, she hadn't been able to stop thinking about it.

"More than thinking, Mark," she said. "I'm really considering it."

He reached over and touched her arm, then pulled his hand back to the steering wheel, looking straight ahead. "Well, I hope you don't."

She stared at her arm, the place he'd just touched her, and she made herself reach for her sweater and pull it up. She was suddenly feeling that uncomfortable closeness, the kinds of feelings she couldn't ever have for Mark.

Chapter 12

"Sign here," said the prison guard, then slid a tray through the window. "You'll have to check your gun and personal effects."

Mark signed his name and slid the book over to Billy Jo so she could sign hers as well. He unclipped his holstered gun and tossed it in the tray along with his keys. Billy Jo had left her bag locked in his Jeep after the two-hour drive since the ferry docked, and he thought she had feigned sleep for most of the way.

He didn't know why she seemed suddenly so quiet, so off.

The door buzzed and a guard opened it, and he wondered whether a person could ever get used to the sounds of a prison, the concrete, the bars, the loud buzzing. He motioned for Billy Jo to go first, aware that the chief had apparently made good on his word and reached out to the warden. He was expected.

Billy Jo pulled at her sweater as she looked around, tense, stressed.

"You okay?" He didn't know why he asked, considering he was aware she didn't respond well to anyone thinking she was weak. Being caring or thoughtful as normal people did would have her snarling in response.

"Fine," she snapped. She didn't look his way at first, but then she did. "Sorry, just that I was in a place like this. My dad got me out, and the rest is history…"

She moved ahead of him as the guard opened a door and led them into the jail, down another hallway and past another unlocked door. The scrape of metal was jarring. They stepped into a long and narrow room and were directed to two stools before a glass partition. So this was the big time, where the dangerous offenders were.

There wasn't a lot of room in the cubby, and his leg brushed Billy Jo's. There was no one on the other side, and he would've been a fool to miss how uncomfortable she was.

"You said you pulled a gun at a gas station, and your dad, who adopted you, got you out of jail," he said. "How old were you, again?"

By the way she rolled her shoulders, it was a memory he didn't think she wanted to relive. "Fifteen, in a jail for adults. I think if the average person actually had to spend a day inside, they'd think twice, maybe come up with a better way to help all the small-time kids and adults who do a stupid thing and are suddenly tossed in with hardened criminals."

He wasn't sure what to make of her comment. The door clanged loudly and opened to reveal a man with dark hair, graying at the sides, in a brown jumpsuit. He was led to the stool on the other side of the plexiglass, which had holes in it to talk through. He had brown eyes, and Mark didn't think he was that old.

"Who are you?" He didn't sound friendly.

"I'm Detective Mark Friessen, from Roche Harbor, and this is Billy Jo McCabe, with DCFS. I wanted to talk with you about the case of your daughter, Gabriele. I'm just clearing up some inconsistencies."

For a moment, he thought the man was going to leave.

"I'm done," Brice said. "I'm not talking to you."

"Wait, this is important," Mark said. "This is about your little girl and where her body is."

The man had stood up. He stilled before turning back to Mark and Billy Jo. There was such anger and hate there.

"Sit down, please," Mark said. "I have some questions for you. You were charged with killing your daughter, whom you took. What happened? The chief has said to offer you anything to get you to tell us where she is."

The man sat down. "You think I would kill my little girl? I didn't take her, didn't hurt her. What is it you really want?" His voice was rough, and he had a scar at the side of his neck.

Mark was aware of the sheer number of criminals who screamed they were innocent when they weren't. It was a trap he wasn't walking into. "Look, you're facing a life sentence. You want to be relocated, maybe have a window, get a few years knocked off? You have something to bargain with, you know. You tell me where she is, and I can promise you I'll work with the DA, the warden, to see that something better is negotiated to make your time easier in here."

He wasn't sure whether the man laughed as he lowered his head and shook it, then pulled his hand through his wavy and unkempt hair. "You think I give a shit about that? I'm telling you I didn't take her. I didn't kill my daughter. You want me to lie? Or is it that you want me to say I took her and tell you, what, that I tossed her body in the ocean, took a boat out and dropped her? Yeah, that was the DA's version—but wait, I don't even own a boat. Or how about this one? I hated my ex-wife so much that I took my daughter when she was sleeping and killed her so my wife wouldn't have her. It doesn't matter whether it's the truth; it was believable, and now you want me to tell you where her body is when I didn't kill her. Where is Detective Singer?"

The way he said it, Mark wondered what he was supposed to say.

"He retired. I took over his job on the island. What can you tell me about the domestic dispute call, the fight between you and your wife outside before your daughter went missing?"

He didn't look over to Billy Jo, but he could feel this going in a direction he hadn't expected.

"What?" The man sounded so sarcastic. "You came all the way out here to ask me about that fight?"

"Humor me, will you? Look, the file had a lot of holes in it, and I'm just doing some due diligence because some things don't add up. The fight outside between you and Nia, what was it about? I understand Detective Singer showed up and told you to leave." He wasn't sure Brice was even going to answer him.

"She was having an affair with my best friend and business partner," he finally replied.

"And you hit her," Mark said.

Brice sat up straighter and crossed his arms. His face had the kind of hardened look that every man behind bars seemed to take on. "I didn't hit that bitch. She slapped me, and when she went to hit me again, I pushed her away. Yeah, I called her a lying cunt and told her to get the fuck out and pack her bags, that she'd get nothing from me. I told her she'd never see our daughter again, that I'd see to it she got nothing. Then Detective Singer showed up, tackled me, and cuffed me. After he spoke with Nia, he said he wouldn't press charges against me for domestic abuse if I left.

"Suddenly, I was the one being forced to leave or he'd take me to jail even though Nia was the one who had cheated. She wasn't even a mother to our daughter, never was. I bathed her. I fed her. I took her to daycare, to the doctor. I saw to her every need. And what did Nia do but fuck my partner? Right under my nose. I understand they're both living in my house now. They both have my business, all of it, and what do I have but thirty years because two people I trusted screwed me? And now you're here, wanting me to tell you where my daughter is? Fuck off," he said so calmly. He turned toward the door and called out, "I'm done here!"

A guard appeared.

"Wait. Just give us another minute," Mark yelled at the guard. He stood up, his hand pressed to the plexiglass. "Then tell me why Nia said you did this. She pointed the finger at you, said you had a key to the house, yet the window was open in Gabriele's room. Even your business partner, Dylan, said you did this, and Detective Singer focused only on you."

Brice had taken a step. He turned, looking over his shoulder back to Mark, as the guard said nothing, only waited with his hand on Brice's arm. "You really have no idea, do you, Detective?" he finally said. He said something to the guard, who dropped his hand, and Brice took a step back to the stool and sat down.

"You're right. I don't," Mark said. "So why don't you tell me what I'm missing? Why does your case file have statements from your ex-wife and your business partner saying you took your daughter in retaliation and then killed her? Detective Singer focused only on you, so there has to be more. I have to be missing something." He gestured toward Brice, then realized the man was looking right at Billy Jo, who had said nothing.

"You're right about one thing, Detective," Brice said. "That detective didn't look at anyone but me. I'm suddenly living with my business partner and best friend in his guest room, knowing he's sleeping with my wife and has been for years, yet we're both pretending neither of us knows. You know where that detective found me the night my daughter went missing from her bedroom, from her crib, where she was sleeping? I was passed out cold, drunk. I was yanked from bed, cuffed, and tossed in a cell, and the entire time I was thinking this was just a bad dream I'd wake up from.

"The thing no one wants to talk about is the motive. I loved that little girl. But the night of our fight, when Singer showed up and cuffed me, I'd just found out Gabby wasn't mine. Can you imagine that, Detective, a woman doing that to you? You love a baby and raise her believing she's yours only to learn from a lying bitch that she isn't. That was after I demanded a divorce, told her I'd see to it she got nothing. You know what my lawyer said? That it just gave me a motive and made me look guilty. But my lawyer also said not to worry—no body, no crime. He told me they couldn't charge me, but then suddenly we were at my trial, with no jury, just a judge my lawyer said would toss it out. Now here I am, convicted, just another felon who will never see the light of day. And no one was looking for my little Gabby because everyone said she was dead, yet there's no body."

Mark wasn't sure what to make of him. He'd come for answers, but all he had now were more questions. "So what happened to Gabriele, then? If you didn't take her, who did?"

Brice dragged his gaze from Billy Jo to him and back, sitting up straighter. "Don't know. Can't help you there, Detective. But let me tell you what it's like here, sitting in a box, behind bars, locked up, when I have no idea where my daughter is. Someone took her, and I can't do a damn thing about it. No one will listen. No one is looking for her. You have any idea what that does to a person? It's hell, a living hell. Unless you're about to tell me you're reopening my case, that you're going to look for Gabby, I'd say we're done." He was leaving again.

"So why do you think Detective Singer went after you?" Billy Jo cut in.

He thought Brice smiled. The man dragged his gaze over to Mark and then back, his smile widening, and a laugh bubbled up. "You both really have no idea," he said. He leaned in and shook his head. "Harry Singer is Nia's uncle. They're family."

This time, when Brice got up, Mark felt—and not for the first time—that he was just a player in some game that everyone else knew the rules to, and no one had bothered to tell him. He heard the clang of the door on the other side.

Billy Jo nudged him, as Brice was now gone. "Well, I

guess you won't be getting a confession out of him. I wonder why the chief didn't bother to mention the family connection." She stood up, rested her hand on his shoulder, and squeezed. "Come on, let's go," she said, already at the door and glancing back to him.

He took in the concrete, the loud clanging, the vibration of noise that rocked his senses as he tried to decide what to do next. He reached for Billy Jo's arm and had to look way down at her, as she was so short. "Hey, just hang on a second. If this is true, what happened to that little girl? Who took her?"

She glanced to the steel door as it opened to reveal a guard waiting. Then she looked back up at him. "I don't know, but it seems that just maybe, someone isn't telling the truth. So who do you want to talk to first—the chief, Detective Singer? Or maybe we take this back to Nia and Dylan. I'm not the detective, but just in case you missed what he said about not being Gabriele's father, start there. Who do you think the father is, Mark?"

Then they stepped through the steel door, and he listened to it clang behind him. What if Brice Martin was, in fact, innocent?

Chapter 13

She wondered, if someone like Mark Friessen had been around when she'd been in trouble as a kid, would he have gone the extra mile for her? There was just something about him, his character, who he was, that made her wonder what he would do next. But her expectations of others often left her disappointed.

He held everything in, held his cards close to his chest. She understood clearly that his back was to the wall, and maybe that was why she'd left him to his thoughts, his silence, as he drove.

They had pulled into a drive-through and picked up burgers and fries, and she wasn't sure when he'd flicked his headlights on. As she finished her fries and tucked the wrapper in the paper bag at her feet, his cell phone rang again. He pulled it from his inside pocket and swore under his breath.

"The chief again?" she said, though his pissed-off look said everything.

"Yup," he replied, then silenced the ringer and tucked it back into his jean jacket.

"What is that, like two times now?"

He shook his head. "Three. Can only push this so far before I'll be the one packing my bags and leaving the island, looking for a different line of work."

Something about the way he said it filled her with an ache, a loss, as if something was coming at both of them, an ending to something she wasn't sure she wanted to end.

"What are you going to tell him?" she said.

Mark hit a rut in the road, and she bounced in her seat. Nothing about riding in his Jeep was quiet or smooth. "Haven't figured it out yet, but I need to pretty quickly. Looks like we'll be on the late ferry. You want to stop anywhere?" He looked at his watch, changing the subject so easily.

She shook her head. "No, just keep going. I have to use the bathroom but can wait until we get to the ferry terminal. You've been pretty quiet since we left the jail. Do you have any idea what your game plan is? I'm not pushing, Mark, but you already said the chief wanted a confession. I've thought over the entire meeting at the jail, and either that man behind bars is a fantastic actor, which is entirely possible, or he really didn't do it. How do you suppose the chief will respond to you asking about the family relationship between the former detective and Nia, if it's true?

"I mean, I'm still trying to make sense of the connection between all of them. His lawyer was right to control the evidence about little Gabriele not being his daughter, as that would've been a motive. I wonder who his lawyer was, though, because he got totally screwed, and it sounds as if the lawyer picked a trial by judge instead of by jury. Brice has to be thinking what a mistake that was now, gambling on the fact that a judge would actually take all the circumstantial evidence and toss it out. You should also look into who the judge was."

The way he pulled in a breath sounded too much like frustration to her. At the situation or what, she didn't know. Mark was impossible to read at times. He reached for his takeout coffee, into which he'd dumped three packs of sugar. She wondered how he could drink so much coffee, and the sweetness had to be off the charts. It was something she had noticed about him: He lived on coffee and takeout.

"Sounds like you've had some time to think over there. Maybe you missed your calling. You could've been a lawyer."

She thought of her dad, because those were his words. With everything she'd picked up from watching and listening to him, she knew her dad would always be her first call if something came at her. "Nope," she said. "One lawyer in the family is enough."

He shook his head. "Right, your dad. And I know it. My mom's a lawyer, and my older brother Danny followed in her footsteps." For a moment, she thought he sounded almost homesick.

"If you had a chance to go home, would you?" she said. She didn't know why she wanted to know, but she could feel herself holding her breath. She thought a hint of a smile pulled at his lips.

"Should have, could have, would have is not something I subscribe to, Billy Jo. That ship sailed long ago. I'm here, and my family is safer because of it. Look ahead, not behind you. My father drilled that into me."

She couldn't remember ever feeling so unsettled yet comfortable with someone at the same time. She figured

Mark never shared anything about himself, yet here she was, sitting beside him in his vehicle, seeing a part of him she knew he didn't show anyone.

"Sounds wise," she said.

He laughed. "Yeah, not something anyone would call Jed Friessen, though. Stubborn, protective, a father, a husband. I never told him what happened and why I really left, but I think he knows."

Thoughtful, too. Damn. She made herself look away. "You know, all I've done since we left the jail is go over what Brice said. I mean, can you imagine believing a little girl is yours, raising her, and then finding out she's not? Is it true? Damn cruel, if you ask me, and selfish too. Sounds like that little girl was a pawn for the mother. Did Brice snap?"

Mark had his arm resting on the door, and he pulled his hand across his chin with a scrape of his whiskers. He only shook his head. "Not to take it as far as killing a kid, no. But to take her and disappear, sure…" He took a swallow of coffee, then settled it back in the cup holder in the console. "The chief, I can't quite figure out his role in this. Granted, I've been here before, thinking idealistically that someone in charge would actually want to right the wrong when a cop has bent the rules. But I figured out a long time ago that it's all about perception, and anyone in charge is all about making sure the public never sees just how badly the department has screwed up. An innocent person in jail stays in jail.

"The chief was clear with me: The last thing any department wants is a PR nightmare, with the media saying they made a mistake. Then every case that cop had suddenly falls under the spotlight. So I can say with one hundred percent certainty that the chief knows his detective screwed up or railroaded someone, looked the other way, but he's not going down for this. Do me a favor." He pulled his cell phone from his jacket and handed it to her. "Pull up Carmen's name. Her contact info is in there. Put it on speaker."

She didn't know much about the deputy he worked with. The only times she'd seen her around the island, the woman had never said hi or anything. There was just something about her that Billy Jo couldn't quite figure out. She pressed the number and listened to the ring.

"Zarco." Her voice sounded tired, raspy.

"Carmen, it's Mark. You know what's going on?"

There was silence on the other end for a second. "The chief is on the warpath right now. You know that, right?"

"So you know how Singer was in the chief's office when I walked in this morning?" Mark said, steering with one hand. "I just left the prison after speaking with Brice Martin. The chief wants this wrapped up, to get a confession and come up with the location of the little girl's body so the community can have closure, but I'm thinking this is more so the chief can look like he's going above and beyond."

Billy Jo spotted the sign to the ferry. She didn't know what he was trying to accomplish, and she didn't know what side Carmen would be on. Likely whatever side let her keep her job. Who did she report to? Mark needed to be careful.

"I saw Singer drive off the ferry," she said. "Saw him at your desk today, making calls, when I walked in. So I had an idea already. You get the answers the chief wanted?"

She didn't pull her gaze from Mark. He shook his head. Maybe he was wondering the same thing she was about Carmen.

"Nope, but I have a feeling you already knew that. Did you know Harry Singer is Nia's uncle? Family investigating family. Do I need to ask if the chief knows? Did you know? Brice also just dropped a little bomb on us, saying he'd found out Gabriele wasn't even his."

She didn't know what to expect from Carmen, and she wondered why Mark was calling her when she could go right to the chief.

"This is an island, Mark," Carmen said. "You think the chief doesn't know everyone's relationships? I think you already know the answer. And Singer is still on the island, in case you're wondering."

It wasn't lost on her that Carmen hadn't commented on the little girl not being Brice's. Maybe it was her lack of answer that had Billy Jo just staring at the phone she was holding.

"Carmen, cut the crap," Mark said. "I know you know something, because I can't shake the feeling that it isn't a coincidence that you handed me that box, that file. You wanted me to find it. I think you know more."

Billy Jo knew she was frowning. The ferry terminal was up ahead.

"There was always something off about the case," Carmen said. "The chief never wants this coming back on him, to look bad. You know what I mean. You're on your way back? Pretty sure I saw Singer's car parked in the driveway at Nia and Dylan's. You ever wonder how it was that the wolves circled so easily around Brice Martin?"

Even Billy Jo had the feeling that Carmen had

figured out everything about this case. Why wasn't she saying anything?

"Carmen, I know you don't like to put your neck out, and maybe I'll never understand why, but if you know something about the little girl's disappearance, what happened to her, you have to tell me. Because I'm telling you, what I heard today at that jail…"

"Ever wonder why cops lie about what they know when they interview a suspect?"

"Carmen, what the fuck? It's interrogation tactics. Why are we talking about this?"

Billy Jo was really listening. She heard a sigh on the other end.

"Mark, ask yourself why Singer was suddenly on the ferry and in the chief's office. Someone is scared that you've found out whatever it is about this case that no one is supposed to. Evidently, you're really close. The thing about Harry Singer is that he wasn't always that sloppy. So who do you think gains from Brice being in jail? You're a smart cop, Mark. I know you already spoke with Mavis, who ran the daycare, and Carla, who watched Dylan Parry pick up the little girl. Did you know that Harry Singer also has three grown kids, and only one still lives on the island? No one but you knows what was said between you and Brice at the jail. Not the chief, not Harry, and not Dylan or Nia. You know what I mean."

She wasn't sure she understood, but Mark was shaking his head, pissed off.

"I'm on the next ferry," was all he said.

"That's good. If I were you, Mark, I wouldn't share that with the chief," Carmen said. Then she hung up.

Mark pulled up to the ferry booth and waited behind a car that was paying.

"Is she always that cryptic?" Billy Jo said.

Mark only shook his head. "Yeah, another woman who holds her cards close to her chest."

Billy Jo nodded.

Mark pulled out his wallet, then tapped the steering wheel as they waited. "But at least I have an idea what to do."

"And that is?"

He glanced over to her. "Interrogation, when a cop can lie about anything. If I'm right, then just maybe I'll find out the truth of what really happened."

Chapter 14

Something about this moment told him there was no going back. He sat in his Jeep, taking in the house where he'd been just the day before, where the bitter ex now lived with Brice's former business partner. It was a house that had been the scene of a crime four years earlier, and he was struck now, sitting there in the dark, that not even a crime scene photo existed in the file.

The lights were on in the house, but it was only after nine, and he took in the cars in the driveway: the Mercedes, the blue compact off to the side, and a dark pickup he hadn't seen before. He considered how he was going to play this.

"Well, now or never, I guess." He reached for the handle of his door and pulled.

"Mark, hold up a second." Billy Jo touched his arm, and he turned back to her.

The front door opened, and Harry Singer stepped out.

"Well, how about that? Detective Singer is here,"

Mark said, watching as Nia followed him out of the house and hugged him. Dylan was close behind and shook his hand. "You may want to stay here. Although I'm a cop, you're not, and I seem to be digging myself into something you'll want to stay out of. I should've dropped you off at your car." He went to reach for the handle again.

"No, Mark, don't get out. Stay here. Let's see where the detective goes. Follow him. You can always come back and talk with Nia and Dylan." She looked over to him in the darkened Jeep, and they watched the old detective climb into the pickup and then back out of the driveway. Billy Jo pulled her hand away from his arm. "I just have this feeling I can't shake. I don't know what it's about, but let's just see where he goes."

He didn't know why he was still sitting there, listening to Billy Jo, considering he didn't listen to anyone. But there was something about this pain-in-the-ass woman. He didn't know when their relationship had shifted to that of perfect partners in crime. "And then what? I thought the idea was to talk to Nia and Dylan."

The truck was now pulling away, and he started his Jeep as the house door closed. He didn't turn on his lights as he pulled out on the road and started following the detective.

"Humor me and just follow him," Billy Jo said. "It's too late for him to take a ferry off the island. Then, I don't know, but aren't you kind of just making this all up as you go? I sure am. Sometimes, you can pick up so much more by just watching."

The brake lights ahead of him flickered, and Singer turned left at the stop sign. He was heading away from town.

"You know, in case I didn't say it," Mark said, "thanks for tagging along today, being my backup. If your career in social services doesn't work out, you'd make a great partner in crime, considering I'm likely going to be fired by this time tomorrow." He slowed down and flicked on his headlights, not missing the soft laugh from Billy Jo. It was a sound he hadn't heard before from her. He stayed back as Singer rounded the bend ahead.

"Mark, don't jump all the way to the worst-case scenario. The night's still young, and anything could happen to save your job. I noticed the chief hasn't called again."

Right, not since he'd talked to Carmen. Why couldn't he shake the feeling that she could be playing both sides?

"Up there, he just turned." Billy Jo gestured.

He was struck with the uncomfortable feeling that having Billy Jo there beside him, helping to unravel this twisted web, was the only thing that felt right about this situation. But he couldn't tell her that. As he squeezed the wheel, feeling his life unraveling, his career, he worried he was dragging her into the line of fire. He didn't know how he could be so careless.

He turned the corner and sped up when the truck lights disappeared.

"Where'd he go? Did you see?" She was looking as he drove, then gestured to the side of the road. "Over there, Mark! Down that driveway."

He could see some big homes in the distance through the trees as he pulled down a paved driveway with bushes on each side. He flicked off his lights, seeing the truck pull up in front of a big stone house. The front window was massive, and the stone fireplace went up two stories. Mark turned off the Jeep and just watched as Harry Singer stepped out of his pickup and started to the front door.

It opened before he stepped up onto the big stone step, as the man inside was waiting for him. A little kid ran right out past him and into his arms, and Singer lifted the kid. Maybe a grandkid? It seemed the home-owner knew Singer well and had been expecting him.

"Do you think that's his son? Carmen said one of his grown kids still lives here on the island."

Billy Jo pulled on the door, and the inside light of his Jeep flicked on. "Looks like it, or someone else he's close with. So how about we go say hi and find out?"

He hadn't been planning on this. "Billy Jo, no, wait…" he said as she stepped out.

But she closed the door.

"Dammit!" he snapped, then pulled his keys from the ignition of his Jeep and opened his door to step out into the dark. He shoved it closed and started after Billy Jo, who was heading right to the front door. He reached for her arm. "Wait, wait. Look, we can't just walk up and ring the bell. Then what? Need a plan here, Billy Jo, or he's going to have the chief on the phone before I can figure out anything to ask."

He had pulled her to a stop and felt her arm tense as she turned to him. Her hand rested on his chest, and she patted it. He let her go, unsure of what she was thinking as she shook her head.

"Actually, that's exactly what we're going to do. We're going to knock on the door, and you're going to confront Singer, call him out." She actually reached for his arm and slid her hand around it. He didn't move, though, as he looked down at her. "What did Carmen say? You're a cop, interrogating him. Tell a different story. As I figure it, you have about thirty, forty feet to figure out something before we're at the door. Then let's see where this goes."

She gave his arm a tug and started walking, leaving him no choice but to walk with her to the front door. All he could think was that this girl wasn't scared of anything.

Chapter 15

She figured the property had to be at least two acres. The impressive wood front door was carved with a bear, and the wood columns to either side stood at least two stories. It was the kind of entrance that made a statement as the bell chimed from inside.

There was something about the detective. She'd never for one moment thought he lacked courage, but for the first time she wondered whether he could think as quickly on his feet as she hoped he could.

"You ready for this?" she said.

He just glanced down to her, shook his head, and shrugged, which she took to mean that words wouldn't be forthcoming. She listened to the clang of the bell again and heard the door being unlocked before it was pulled open.

The man inside had light hair and was likely a few years older than her, of average height and build. "Can I help you?"

"Yes, I'm Detective Mark Friessen. I understand Harry Singer is staying here."

The man stepped back and opened the door. "Yeah, of course. Come in. Dad!" he called out.

Mark gestured for her to go in first. The well-lit entryway was paved with stone that resembled marble, with a deep blue and gold area rug overtop. She took in her image in the floor-to-ceiling mirrors behind the long hall table.

"Detective," said an older man who appeared from somewhere in the house. He had thinning hair brushed back and was not that tall, round in the middle. There was something about putting a face to the name. Billy Jo found herself looking up the large staircase, taking in the second level. So this was the detective and his family.

Interesting.

"What are you doing here?" Singer said. "How did you know I'd be here?"

"Was hoping we could have a moment to talk. And you forget I'm a cop. It wasn't that hard to find you. Didn't realize you had family on the island, a son. You must spend a lot of time coming back and forth."

Billy Jo thought she heard voices, and she noticed a woman with tied-back brown hair, a little soft in the middle, wearing glasses.

"Oh, didn't know someone was here," she said. "Harry, are you still putting the kids to bed?"

Billy Jo let her gaze linger on the mail on the table. Abe Singer was the name she saw. She forced a smile to her lips.

"Glenda, it'll have to wait a bit," Singer said. "Why don't you take the kids up? I'll be up to read them a story as soon as I'm done here."

She realized everyone was looking at her now. "Hi, I'm Billy Jo. I'm with Mark," she said. She didn't miss the odd look on Mark's face, but she didn't think adding her DCFS title would do anything other than have them shown the door.

She heard giggling and saw two kids running past Glenda, who had to be their mother. Singer was related to this family.

"So what's going on?" Glenda asked, not saying anything more about putting her kids to bed. "Joanny, Tara, stop running! Go put your toys away," she called out and actually clapped her hands.

Billy Jo took a step forward. In the front living room, the kids were jumping amid toys that appeared spread out everywhere.

"Just have some questions, is all," Mark said. "Harry, wonder if I could have a word with you about Brice. Saw him at the jail today. I didn't realize Nia was your niece."

Billy Jo didn't miss the exchange between Glenda and Abe. Harry Singer, though, had his hands in his pockets. Billy Jo took another step, standing in the opening to the living room. The kids were picking up toys and tossing them in the bin. How old were they? Five, maybe six?

"What does Nia being our cousin have to do with anything?" Abe said. "What's going on here, Dad?"

Billy Jo realized everyone was looking at Mark, not really noticing her as she slipped into the living room and over to the kids. She could hear Mark still talking as she crouched down and said in a low voice, "Hi, what's your name?"

The kids had light hair, shoulder length, and round

cheeks, already in their pajamas. They appeared almost the same height.

"I'm Joanny," said one.

"Tara," said the other with a little jump.

"How old are you?" Billy Jo said.

Tara held up three fingers.

"I'm five years old," Joanny said.

"This is Bunny." Tara held up a floppy brown stuffed rabbit.

"Oh, he's so cute. Is he yours?"

The little girl nodded. She seemed so damn happy, the kind of happiness Billy Jo never saw in the kids she was called to protect. By the time she was there, she saw only the kind of fear and shock that should never be in a kid's eyes. "So you get to have time with Grandpa?" she said.

"Yeah, I like it when he comes to see us. He plays with us, and he said he'd take us on his boat."

She could still hear the talking in the entryway, and she wondered how long it would be until someone realized she was in there, talking to the girls. So Harry had a boat. "Does your grandpa take you out on his boat lots? I can't remember ever being on someone's boat other than the big noisy ferry."

"Uh-uh," Joanny said. "Grandpa only took us out once in the summer. But we're going back with Grandpa on the big ferry boat."

What was it about family? Kids told people everything.

"Do you go over to see your grandpa very often? I don't have a grandpa, so I never had one I got to visit."

"Grandpa lives with his sister, Auntie Beth. He said it's a small house and not as big as ours."

So he lived with his sister. Odd. She wondered whether that was Nia's mother. "So your grandpa's sister's name is Beth? Does your grandpa have any other brothers and sisters like you and Tara have each other? Maybe you two can live together when you grow up."

Her knees were beginning to ache where she squatted on the floor. She reached for some plastic toys and put them in the toy box, then picked up a picture book from the couple on the floor.

"No, Grandpa said he's set in his ways, and so is Aunt Beth," Joanny said. "Grandpa said Aunt Beth makes too many cookies and he's getting fat."

"Yeah, cookies will do that. Bet your grandpa loves his sister cooking just for him."

"She makes the cookies for Shauna, but we're not supposed to tell anyone that. Grandpa sneaks them," Tara whispered to her.

So who was Shauna?

"What's going on here?" said Glenda, standing in the living room entrance, Mark behind her. "Girls, come on. Your grandpa's going to read to you. Hurry, put away all these toys, everything."

The smile Glenda offered to her was anything but warm, and she could feel the tension. She stood up and held the small picture book, which seemed a little worn. She flicked it open to see lambs and what looked like a church. She took in the name written in pen, *Gabriele Martin, my little Gabby*, and the date. Then she closed it up.

"Is this yours?" She held it out to Joanny, who grabbed it to toss it in the toybox.

"No, Grandpa said that's one of Shauna's."

Glenda said nothing as she stood with her arms crossed.

"Billy Jo, ready?" Mark said, lingering, tall, rugged. She was beginning to feel too comfortable with him.

"Yeah," Billy Jo said. "Nice to meet you, Glenda. You have cute kids."

Glenda only nodded.

Billy Jo stepped over to Mark and took in the old detective standing with his hand protectively over the girls, who were leaning against him. The son, Abe, had pulled open the door. She kept walking out onto the big stone step, and then she could feel Mark behind her. He fell in beside her as the door closed.

"So what did you learn?" she asked him.

All he did was shake his head. "Nothing, just that his son Abe and his wife, Glenda, live here with their two kids. He comes over often. The pool and spa business Brice Martin owned with Dylan Parry hadn't turned a profit in five years. When I told him Brice actually had an alibi the night little Gabriele disappeared, Harry laughed and called me out. The man gave nothing, and his son said nothing either. So I decided to add in some of the truth I'd learned. I asked Harry outright if he knew whether Brice was Gabriele's biological father, that he'd just found out he wasn't. Harry gave nothing away, but his son sure seemed uncomfortable. When I asked if they knew who the father was, Harry said it was time for us to leave. This web seems to be unravelling, but the problem is that time is running out for me. I guess the only thing I can do is head back over to Nia and Dylan's, see what I can get, but I'm not sure what my next move is."

She could see his Jeep just ahead. "Well, while you

were getting stonewalled, I met his granddaughters. The thing about kids is that they haven't learned to evade and lie like adults yet. Did you know Detective Singer lives with his sister, Beth, and Beth bakes cookies for someone named Shauna? As I was helping the girls clean up their toys, I saw that one of the picture books there had Gabriele's name in it. Joanny, the eldest, said her grandpa said the book was Shauna's."

Mark rested his hand on the hood of his Jeep and looked down at her. She could see the minute he understood what she was saying, and he pulled his hand roughly over his face. "I swear, Billy Jo, this is more fucked up than I realized."

What could she say to that? "So now what?"

He was still looking at the house behind him. Then he looked back to her. "We pay a visit to Beth Singer. I think it's time to find out what Harry Singer is really hiding."

His cell phone started ringing, and when Mark reached for it in his jacket pocket and stared at it a second before answering, she didn't have to ask who it was.

"Hi, Chief. I guess you'd like to know why I haven't called you back and why I'm standing outside Harry Singer's son's place after a very enlightening visit with Brice Martin. You know what I learned? Not only did Brice have an alibi the night his daughter was taken and supposedly killed, but he'd just found out Gabriele wasn't even his. And imagine my surprise when I learned that Singer is Nia's uncle."

She just stared in horror, but she also wanted to reach out to Mark and pat him on the back, He stood there, staring at her, and she was unsure of what the chief was yelling at him. He pulled the phone away from his ear and let out a rough sigh before holding it up.

"He hung up on me," he said, then shook his head, looking over her into the dark. When he looked back to her, he said, "But not before telling me I'm fired."

Chapter 16

The case was over.

He sat in the cold outside, picturing the file, now sealed and likely shoved into that storage unit with so many other cold and closed cases. It left him with a sick feeling.

He listened to the dog's nails scraping on the wooden deck as he sat in a folding camp chair that had seen better days. The sun was coming up, and the silence of the morning was usually something he welcomed, but not today.

"Here, looks like you could use this. Black in the morning, right?"

He took in the coffee that appeared beside him in an old mug. It was steaming, offered by a slender hand. There were her freckles, her determined blue eyes.

"Yeah, thanks," he said.

Billy Jo strode across his deck, a blanket pulled over her shoulders, also holding a mug of coffee. She walked right to the edge. The wooden deck didn't have a rail, so she just stood there with her back to him, watching the sun come up.

"You could have gone home last night, you know," he said.

She didn't turn around. As he took in her Nissan, an odd shade of green, shiny and new, parked next to his black Jeep, he wondered where he was supposed to go next.

"Right," she said. "As if, Mark, considering I likely had a hand in getting you fired. As you once said to me, friends don't desert friends when they're down and out. Last night, sorry to say, you had the rug yanked out from under you because you were trying to do the right thing."

He wasn't sure what to say, so he said nothing, taking in how ridiculous she looked, her hair a mess, wearing yesterday's clothes under that old blanket.

"You sat out here all night, didn't you?" she said.

What was he supposed to say to that? She'd taken his bed, and he'd been planning on the sofa but had found himself still outside at dawn, watching the sun come up. He had no idea what time it was.

"You know, Mark, I'm about the worst person to carry a conversation. I thrive on uncomfortable silences." She looked away again, her back to him. The mangy mutt wandered over to her and lay down at her feet, and she bent down with her coffee and pet him. "So what's the plan this morning?" She stood up and faced him, pulling the blanket again and taking a swallow of coffee, steaming from the morning chill.

He should've been cold, but the heavy coat he'd pulled on before coming out the night before had kept him reasonably comfortable. "Well, I'll likely have to turn over my badge and my service revolver." But not the gun he kept under his pillow, the one he slept with, which would always be his. "And then I guess I'll figure out what's next on the horizon. After this time, my chances of getting hired on as a cop anywhere have dropped to near zero. This place is paid up till the end of the month, but I'll need to give notice. Maybe I'll head to North Lakewood, see my folks, my family, for a bit. Then I'll figure out what my future holds."

She was still looking at him when he heard a vehicle. When he spotted the sheriff's car pulling in and parking, he didn't bother sitting up.

Billy Jo glanced at it. "Did you know Carmen was coming over?"

He only shook his head. "Nope."

She didn't look his way again, and he watched as the deputy stepped out of her car. She closed the door, already dressed in a uniform, her dark hair pulled back. She had sunglasses on and didn't pull them off until she started walking their way. Then she tucked them in her zipped jacket as she nodded to Billy Jo and stepped up on the deck. The dog sat up but stayed next to Billy Jo.

"Carmen, what are you doing here?" Mark said.

She was looking at his cabin and then past him, likely to the open door. Then she let her gaze settle on him. "Heard what happened."

He just lifted the coffee, which he welcomed, and took another swallow. He didn't pull his gaze from her.

"You should know that the chief is now officially looking into the Martin case," she said, shoving her hands in her pockets.

He wasn't sure what to say to Carmen. He had the feeling she knew so much more about this case than he did, and he couldn't figure out why she was holding back. "Good, but not sure how that has anything to do with me. As you know, I've been fired, so I'm no longer a cop. With that title goes the power that comes along with the badge. I'm now just a regular Joe, with all the limited rights that go with that. Did the chief send you here to pick up my badge, my gun?"

Carmen dragged her gaze over to Billy Jo, and he wondered whether she was going to ask her to give them a minute alone. "The chief doesn't know I'm here, but you should know that Harry Singer walked into the office before I left this morning. Never heard the chief yell like that. Have never seen him so volatile before. Listen, Mark, there are some things about the chief that I'm sure you know. He may have wondered about this case, but when the DA charged Brice and the judge convicted him, the chief took the win and told Harry to file it. He wanted you to get a confession so he could tell the people of the island that there was closure, that the little girl's body had been found. Then he'd look like he did his job. Now, instead, he has a shitstorm at his door that he knows I set in motion."

He wasn't sure he'd heard right.

Carmen continued. "I told the chief I was the one who made sure you saw the file because I know what a good cop you are. I also told the chief something you don't know: The reason Brice Martin had to go is that he discovered Dylan Parry had been using the hot tub business to smuggle cocaine, filling the tubs and shipping them. Brice had found out. The entire failing business was a front for the transport of illegal drugs. Nia was having an affair with Dylan, and the baby wasn't Brice's…"

He just stared at her. He wasn't sure what to make of Billy Jo's expression, either.

She didn't pull her gaze from Carmen as she said, "You knew all of this and didn't bother telling Mark? You had him chasing his tail to figure out something you already knew? So you know who Gabriele's father is? Do you know what really happened to her?"

There was something about the snarl that often came from Billy Jo. He realized that was one of two modes she operated from, being under attack or defending someone. She was a mystery, and he was glad that right now, she was on his side.

"I know Harry would do anything to protect Nia," Carmen said. "When the little girl went missing, Harry was the first on the scene, and I was the second, with the chief. I knew the moment I walked in that the mom was high. Harry did, too. She had sampled the product Dylan brought over. When I mentioned it to him, Harry told me to forget I saw it. I always suspected something else had happened. I was the one who told Harry about the tip I'd received about the cocaine in the hot tubs. He said he'd take care of it. When this all went down, I asked Harry about the drugs while Brice was being charged. He said my tip was wrong, that he'd checked but there hadn't been any drugs. I knew he was lying, but I had no proof. I told the chief everything this morning, right before Harry showed up, demanding your head on a spike. He's scared."

Mark only pulled in a breath, wondering why Carmen hadn't told him this to begin with. He realized now what he was seeing. "So what happened to you? You didn't pursue this case. Instead, you made sure I was the one sticking my neck on the line, hoping to solve a mystery that has too many holes in it. The only way for justice to be served is to toss out the entire case and start over. So why? Seriously, Carmen, I want to know."

Carmen stilled and pulled in a breath. Then she turned to look at Billy Jo, letting her gaze linger.

"You know what?" Billy Jo said. "I have to go to the bathroom."

He hadn't expected that from her. He watched as she strode back into the house, giving Carmen the privacy he hadn't wanted her to give.

"I'm waiting," he said. "What gives? What happened to you?"

"You may have been fired, Mark, but I would've been put in jail," she said.

He didn't know what she was talking about. He just shrugged and shook his head.

"Once upon a time, I had a kid," she said. "His name is Dillan. He was six when he was taken from me because of a doctor. He had a cold, you know, the flu kids get, but his cough got worse. I took him to a family doctor at a clinic, who said it was just a bad cold, not to worry about it, to give him fluids and let him rest. But then his cough was so bad he couldn't breathe. I took him to emergency, and the doctor on call called social services on me, citing neglect, saying I hadn't provided proper care. He had pneumonia, the kind he could get only from neglect. The social worker was already there.

"When the doctor told me the diagnosis, I was dragged out of the room by security. They took my kid, pumped him full of drugs, and put him in care. A bogus claim, sure, but how could I prove it? Of course, I figured the doctor had taken one look at the color of my skin and assumed the worst. I wasn't heard, and then no one would listen to me. I couldn't afford a lawyer, but I managed to call my sister in Oregon, who I barely know.

"When a hearing was scheduled, and I finally had the opportunity to speak, I realized no one had bothered to talk to the family doctor. So I paid him a visit, of course, an angry single mother, and all it accomplished was for me to have the chief called on me by the nurse out front. I was handcuffed for the disturbance, for civil disobedience, and was taken to jail. But the doctor asked the chief to drop the charges. The chief just told me to clean up my act.

"My sister now has custody of my son. I'm not sure whether the chief took pity or really understood what had happened, but he hired me, trained me, and I learned that the rules the world operates on are really a mirage. I'm sorry, Mark, but sticking my neck out for someone has left me with my head on the chopping block too many times. I won't do it. But did Brice Martin kill that little girl? I know Harry Singer made sure the case was handled and closed."

He didn't know what to say to Carmen. He was still angry.

"I don't think the little girl is dead," Carmen finally said.

Mark lifted his gaze to her when he heard a creak. He turned to see Billy Jo in the doorway.

"Harry lives with a sister, Beth," Mark said. "How hard would we have to dig to find out that she's Nia's mother?"

Carmen said nothing, then pulled her hand over her face.

"She bakes cookies for a child named Shauna," Billy Jo added.

Carmen was nodding. "One thing about the chief, Mark: He shoots from the hip at times, but Gail has always been his voice of reason. Harry Singer lives in Astoria with his sister. The house is in her name, and she lives mortgage free. You should talk to the chief, and then you should pay Beth a visit."

His cell phone was ringing. He could hear it from inside. Billy Jo walked in and grabbed it, then appeared beside him and held it out, saying, "The chief is calling you."

It rang again. He just lifted his gaze and took it, then pressed it to his ear. "Chief, what can I do for you?" he said. He was still reclining in the deck chair, while Billy Jo walked over to Carmen.

"It's Gail," said the woman on the other end. "I need you to get in here, Mark. Tolly has some things to handle, and you have a job to do."

He pulled the phone away and stared for a second, then pressed it to his ear again. "He fired me," he said.

He wasn't sure what sound she made on the other end, but he thought she swore. "No, you're not fired. Now get your ass in here. Dylan and Nia are on their way in, and you need to take their statements. And tell Carmen, who I know is at your place, that she's on phones. I expect to see both of you in fifteen."

Then she hung up, and he pulled the phone away, taking in the two women who were staring at him. For the life of him, he didn't know what the hell had just happened.

Chapter 17

He was staring at the station's older flatscreen TV, seeing the newsreel with the byline "Gabriele Martin found alive."

He didn't think he'd ever forget the moment he'd heard from the chief that he, along with the Astoria police, had discovered Gabriele Martin living with her grandmother under an assumed identity, Shauna Singer.

She wasn't dead. The news showed footage of former detective Harry Singer and his sister, Beth, being handcuffed by the Astoria police, led to a police car, and put in back. Then came an image of the three-thousand-square-foot house, paid for with the proceeds of crime. Nia and Dylan had also been charged with trafficking and smuggling.

He knew the DA wasn't looking too good in the public eye.

The attorney general had even weighed in with a statement, and the defence attorney who'd represented Brice Martin also took his ten minutes of glory in the media. Brice would be released by the end of the week.

"Mark, turn it up so we can hear it!" Gail called out from behind him as she cleaned the mugs and coffeepot.

He watched the chief appear on the TV, another news conference. The island, which had been rocked with the scandal four years earlier, was now in the spotlight again. He pressed the volume on the remote and turned it up, then tossed it on his desk.

"Good evening, everyone," the chief said. "First off, I want to extend my deepest apologies to Brice Martin for the charges against him and for the four years he's spent in jail for a crime he didn't commit. I can assure you the Roche Harbor Police Department takes this case seriously, and we are deeply disturbed that former detective Harry Singer not only falsified records but saw to it that an innocent man was railroaded and charged with a crime.

"The department, as you know, brought in Detective Mark Friessen to take over from Detective Singer, and with his exemplary record and skills, he uncovered this miscarriage of justice. Detective Friessen, with the full support of this office, discovered that this case was linked to one of the largest narcotics smuggling rings in this part of the Pacific Northwest. Although we can't give Mr. Martin back his four years, this office extends our deepest apologies and plans to reunite father and daughter in the coming days."

Mark leaned against his desk as the reporters yelled out questions, knowing the only reason he still had a job was because it was the only way for the chief to look good, not because he had done the right thing.

"Mark, you did good," said Gail, tapping his shoulder. She stopped in front of him, and something about the way she'd said it and looked at him made him wonder who really ran the department.

At the same time, they still didn't know who Gabriele Martin's biological father was, and he wondered whether that question would ever be answered.

He took in Carmen at her desk, sifting through files. He wasn't sure what to say to her.

Then the front door to the sheriff's office opened, and there was Billy Jo, wearing that same brown cardigan she always wore. Her gaze reached over to him.

"Billy Jo, what are you doing here?" Gail called out to her.

Billy Jo smiled, something she rarely did, as she gestured toward him. "Just here to have a word with the detective."

He didn't move from where he leaned against the desk, thankful when Gail took the remote and turned the sound down on the TV, the fifteen minutes of fame the chief was getting.

"You have time for coffee?" Billy Jo said.

He lifted his mug, which had coffee in it, and she just rolled her eyes.

"I mean for me," she added.

"Sure, as long as it's not the coffeehouse," he said. He'd burned that bridge and was seeing Sybil only from a distance now.

Billy Jo said nothing for a second, then gave her head a shake. Of course, she knew, and he appreciated not having to elaborate or have questions about what the hell he was thinking thrown in his face.

He gestured to the door, and she pulled it open and

strode out. Carmen looked over to him, while Gail was now at her desk, so he called out, "I'm heading out. I have my cell phone if something comes up."

He didn't wait for anyone to answer as he stepped out of the office and pulled the door closed, taking in the street and following Billy Jo. She stopped beside her car, which was parked now beside his Jeep.

"So what's up?" he said.

"You know how I was considering leaving, looking for another job?" She looked away, and his stomach knotted.

"And?" He didn't want her to go.

"It appears I'm stuck for now. Put in a request, but it was denied until they can find someone to take my job. It looks like I'm staying."

He pulled in a breath and took in how awkward she seemed. "If I tell you I'm happy that you're staying, will you take it the wrong way?"

She lifted her gaze, those blue eyes. She was real in a way no one he'd ever met before was. Her look wasn't sassy or flirtatious. She was a girl who could tell him right where to go and give him directions without blinking an eye. He could feel his smile widen.

"You aren't going to get all mushy, are you?" she said. There it was, the snarl. He just loved that about her.

He laughed as he shook his head. "Not with you. You'd likely slug me. So, coffee at the hotel?"

"Yeah, since you kind of ruined the coffeehouse for me, too, because you just couldn't stop yourself from messing around with the girl who runs it." She fell in beside him as they crossed the road to the hotel.

"I never told you I was perfect," he said.

She looked up at him and shook her head. "No, just deeply flawed and screwed up—and who isn't, Mark?"

She stopped at the door to the hotel restaurant as a couple walked out, and she nodded to them with a smile before stepping in as he held the edge of the door over her head.

He just took in this pain-in-the-ass misfit, who had tested him in so many ways but, at the end of the day, was the first person he had really ever been able to depend on. He wondered at what point that had changed, morphing her into someone he saw as more than a friend.

"You want to grab some lunch too?" he said.

She shrugged and made a face. "Why not?"

Yeah, Billy Jo McCabe really wasn't like anyone he'd ever met.

The Dinner

Billy Jo pulled the keys from her bag and shoved them in her mailbox, hearing the chatter around her and doing her best to ignore everyone. She couldn't help but look over her shoulder again before looking back to the empty mailbox, though.

When she closed it up and turned, she took in the dark-haired woman opening the box behind hers, wearing a deputy's uniform. She knew who it was, Carmen, a woman she'd had many reservations about but now understood so much better, as often happened when she took the time to understood what had happened to make a person the way she was and why she did what she did.

She should leave her alone, knowing that was all the woman really wanted, yet Billy Jo found herself waiting for Carmen to close her mailbox. When she turned, her unsmiling dark eyes unnerved her.

"Hi, Carmen. Thought that was you," she said, though she wasn't known for being chatty.

Carmen said nothing at first. "Can I help you with

something?" she finally replied. Right to the point, something she appreciated, but she figured Carmen was just as likely to walk around her and out the door.

Billy Jo nodded to the postal worker behind the counter, who was looking their way, then turned back to Carmen. "I just wanted to ask you about Brice Martin. Heard he was released the other day. I expected some news about his little girl, Gabriele. I know social services in Astoria had her, but I wonder if Brice is coming back here or…"

She could have asked Mark, but Mark was being Mark again, and she hadn't seen or heard from him since their coffee at the hotel. She couldn't shake a feeling that had scared the shit out of her, the feeling that they had suddenly and unexpectedly crossed the line from friendship, shifting into something different. It was nothing she could put her finger on.

"I have no idea," Carmen said, giving her nothing. She shook her head and started walking to the door, away from her.

Billy Jo took in the postal clerk, who was watching them and likely picking up on what wasn't being said. She made herself take a step, seeing Carmen already outside, walking away. She was fast, and Billy Jo had to hurry before she crossed the street.

"Carmen, wait!" she called out. She could see the woman wasn't interested in having personal time with anyone, but she only shook her head when Billy Jo fell in beside her as she started across the street.

"What is it? What do you want?"

"Look, Carmen, I'm not being nosy. I'm just…"

"Yes, you are, so what do you want?"

Just then, Mark drove past them in his Jeep and pulled in front of the station. So much for discretion!

"Mark told you, didn't he?" Carmen said, her anger spewing.

It took Billy Jo a second to understand what she was saying.

"Mark? No, he told me nothing, and I wasn't eavesdropping—but I couldn't help but overhear. I presume we're talking about your kid, who's now living with your sister? Mark doesn't talk about anyone, you know. Of all his faults, that's not one. Besides, you forget what I do. Seriously, Carmen, if there was a way I could help you extract your pound of flesh for what happened, what was taken from you, I would. The system screwed up, and you got screwed. If you want help with anything on that front, just ask."

Carmen dragged her gaze over Billy Jo before making a rude noise under her breath and looking away. "I don't need or want your help."

Point taken!

"Fine, I get it," Billy Jo said. "What are you doing for dinner tonight?"

In response, Carmen froze just as they had crossed the road. She turned and looked down on Billy Jo, who figured Carmen was inches taller than her. Talk about keeping her cards close to her chest. Billy Jo had thought she held the corner on that.

Mark had climbed out of his Jeep and dragged his sunglasses off, not pulling his gaze from them.

"You want to have dinner with me?" Carmen said. Why did it sound like an accusation?

"Unless you have plans or are busy?"

This was generally where someone filled the silence

by saying yes, she did have plans. But Billy Jo would've been surprised if Carmen did, considering she was more of a loner than anyone she'd ever met.

"What's going on here?" Mark said, striding over.

Carmen hesitated and then looked up as if trying to think of a way to tell her no. More than likely, she'd just walk away.

"Carmen and I were just making plans for dinner tonight," Billy Jo said. "I'll put a casserole in the oven. Why don't you come over after your shift, say, six?"

Mark dragged his gaze from her to Carmen and back. His expression was priceless.

"Fine," was all Carmen said before walking away.

Mark actually turned and watched her head inside the sheriff's office before looking back to her. "Didn't know you two were friends," he said. He was kidding, right?

"We're not, but I figured since I'm staying on the island for now, I'd like to know more about some people here."

Mark squinted one eye. The sun had peeked from behind a cloud. He was evidently thinking too much, and there was that distance between them again. One step forward, five back. "Listen, I know I've been kind of scarce lately…"

She waited for him to say something about the fact that she hadn't called him and he hadn't called her, because the way he smiled at her, the way he looked at her, was not the way a friend did.

"We're not dating, Mark," she said. "You don't need to explain something that isn't my business." There she went, closing the door completely—and there was that smile, the humor at her expense.

"So why Carmen?" Maybe it was the way he said it that had her wondering whether he thought this was something else.

"Is there something you want to ask me, Mark?"

He stilled and pulled his gaze, gave his head a shake, and went to step back. "Nope, not asking anything, not my business. You have a great day, Billy Jo."

She didn't know why, but this felt so much like the door being slammed shut, as if she'd been the one to close it. He took another step back to walk away.

"Before you go, you hear anything about Brice Martin?" she said. "Is he planning on coming back to the island? I know child services in Astoria have Gabriele. Has he said anything about taking her, getting custody of her?"

Mark turned back to her.

"I was just asking Carmen, but Carmen being Carmen, she isn't too interested," she continued. "When I reached out to child services in Astoria, they said she's been placed with a family, and no one has any information on the father."

They had also told her that it wasn't in her jurisdiction to ask.

Mark leveled his gaze on her, and it softened even though she could still feel the wall being resurrected between them. He shook his head. "No idea. Not sure he'd want to come back here, considering, and as far as the little girl, she's not even his."

"On paper she is, on the birth certificate. Mark, really? If you raise a little girl, even after being separated this long, you can't turn your feelings off, or I hope you wouldn't."

There was something about Mark. When he looked

at her with those blue unsmiling eyes, the way he was right now, she didn't know what was coming. He was not an easy man to read. "So is this more about you, then?"

She fisted her hands and pulled at her cardigan, wondering how Mark could make her feel so on edge at times. "If it is? I just want a happy ending for that little girl, because out of this fucked-up mess, everyone seems to forget about her. She was just a baby, a toddler, when her dad was taken from her. Then she was living with her grandmother, suddenly no longer called Gabriele but a new name, Shauna.

"Now the only woman she's ever known, the one she's bonded with, is gone, taken from her, because she was part of that sick mess of faking her death so Brice Martin would be out of the picture. Gabriele is innocent, so yes, maybe I want to know that she'll have someone and not become another statistic. Because as hard as I fight for them, this system isn't known for turning out well-adjusted kids. All too often, they become a meal ticket for some adult. So yes, Mark, this is about me and the fact that I'd like to know at least one kid has some chance at normalcy."

Billy Jo could feel her insides shaking, the passion oozing. She was still thinking, too, of Jay Turner, the little boy she hadn't been able to find anyone for here on this island. No one would give a damn and just do the right thing for him.

"You ever find someone to take that little boy with the medical condition?" Mark said. How was it that he seemed to know what she was thinking?

She just shrugged and shook her head. "Sometimes I really hate this job."

He reached over and touched her shoulder. It was

kind, the Mark she was familiar with. He sighed and looked over her head. "Why don't I do some digging and find out what plans Brice has? Let's say I'll show up for that casserole you're planning for Carmen, so make extra."

It was something she hadn't expected. Then he was walking away, and he glanced back to her just once before opening the door to the sheriff's office and walking in.

Damn, there it was again, that awkwardness, that look she didn't think she could handle when all she wanted was for the line of friendship to stay firmly entrenched, where it was. Because anything more than that with a man like Mark would be a sure-fire way to a broken heart.

Chapter 19

"She knows something," Carmen said.

Mark hesitated only a second as he poured coffee into his favorite green mug. Carmen stood right there, dumping sugar and milk into hers, and by the way she said it, she was rattled.

No, she was furious.

"Who are we talking about?" Mark slid the coffeepot back on the burner.

Carmen reached for it and poured, slopping a bit over the side onto the counter. Then she slammed it back on the burner with a clatter, not her usual reserved, calm self. "That nosy friend of yours, Billy Jo."

Huh!

"Maybe you should elaborate, because it seems I missed the first part of this conversation. What are we talking about? She knows something about what? Did she say something to you? I was kind of wondering what that was about out there between you two."

Her eyes widened, and she stilled, looking at him. He realized he'd missed more than a little. He'd thought it was odd to see Billy Jo and Carmen together as he drove up. Evidently, something was going on behind the scenes.

"I shared some pretty personal stuff with you, which wasn't an invitation for you to open your mouth," Carmen said. When he pulled his mug away to reply, she lifted her hand, giving him the flat of it like a punch to the face. "And don't even start about how you shared nothing with no one." Her voice was low, but the bite was there.

She glanced once over her shoulder to Gail, who was going through files, reading something, but then lifted her gaze to them. Evidently, she had her eye on them and was likely wondering what they were talking about.

"I'm very well aware that she was listening when I spilled my guts at your house. You think I like having someone dig around in my past, my business?"

There was the hurt. This was something he hadn't expected from Billy Jo.

"I'll talk to her," he said. "I didn't expect her to say anything. That's not like her. So why did she bring it up? We're talking about your kid, right?"

She pulled in a breath, and he was positive he saw her hand shake. "Yeah, and for the record, I don't need her help."

Apparently, Billy Jo had treaded into Carmen's no-go territory. Maybe he would have a talk with her.

"So she offered to help you with…" He let it hang, lifting his mug, keeping his back to Gail as he took a swallow.

"Anything to do with my kid, but I don't want any more spotlights shining there. And now I'm supposed to show up at her place for dinner?" She made a rude noise.

He could see that Carmen lived in the shadows, hiding from everyone. He wondered whether her unease was more about the fact that Billy Jo was dragging her from that place where she hid from everyone.

"If you don't want to go for dinner, don't go. But if Billy Jo offered to help in some way, you have nothing to lose, Carmen. She has the resources, and she wouldn't go in and do something to hurt you. She has a way about her, and she understands more than you'd think. She has her own experiences of living through the worst kinds of things, things no one should have to. So she knows. You should talk to her. She may surprise you with what an ally she can be."

Carmen had a way of not smiling when she was looking at him. He could see the hurt that was buried so deep, which kept everyone away from her. "You're trying to sell me on her, seriously? Don't. She's your friend, but whatever's going on between you two, I don't want her sticking her nose in my personal life."

He wasn't sure what to make of her comment. Carmen was anything but chatty, and it seemed Billy Jo had managed to scrape open a very raw wound, one she wasn't ready to reveal to anyone.

"I'm not sure what you're referring to," Mark said. "Billy Jo and I are only friends. I'm not her keeper, Carmen, so you may want to tell her all that yourself."

As Carmen stirred her coffee, she gave a shake of her head, and after taking another second to dump her spoon into the sink, she looked up at him. "That is bull-shit. You want to keep telling yourself that you two are just friends, fine, but we all see it even though you both try to pretend there isn't something there. I'm sure you could find another coffee girl to mess around with until you burn that bridge, as well, all the while trying to deny there's something between you and Billy Jo."

He should've said something to clear the air, like that she wasn't his type, that it wasn't that way between them. Except when the rug had been yanked out from under him, and when he found himself with his back against the wall, it had always been Billy Jo who was there.

"You're mistaking a partner in crime and good friend for something more. She has her stuff she's dealing with, and I have mine. By the way, about dinner at Billy Jo's tonight, don't look so worried. I already invited myself, too. Besides, she wants to know about what happened to that little girl, to make sure her life isn't suddenly going to be worse because doing the right thing meant taking Gabriele from her grandmother, the only home she's known, and sticking her somewhere with a bunch of strangers. I told her I would check into it, see what I can find out, check whether Brice plans to take her or leave her in the system."

Mark found himself looking over his shoulder to Gail, who was writing something in a file.

"You two done gossiping over there?" Gail called over. Evidently, she didn't miss anything.

"Nope. Just need to cover the weather, the latest dirt on the island…"

The chief's wife didn't seem impressed as she looked up. "Well, Tolly is on his way in, so I'll be leaving soon. Mark, you still need to make sure your reports are finished and turned in. Carmen, you need to get out there and do rounds."

There were the orders. Carmen took a swallow of her coffee and walked back to her desk, reached for her coat, and shrugged it on. She was quiet, only nodding to Gail as she reached for her keys. So she was just going to walk out.

"See you for dinner tonight, Carmen," he called out.

She paused at the door, and he didn't miss the way Gail looked over to him. Good. So apparently she hadn't heard, by the way she dragged her gaze back and forth between them. Carmen only shook her head as she stepped out and closed the door behind her.

"Didn't know you and Carmen hung out together," Gail said. "Thought that was just something you and Billy Jo did."

He'd just taken a swallow of his coffee, and he choked and coughed. His fisted his hand and pounded his chest, taking in the mischief that appeared in Gail's expression as she held her mug of coffee between two hands.

"Oh, boy, you really have it bad," she said.

"What the hell are you talking about?"

She smiled, and for a moment he didn't think she'd answer. "You and Billy Jo…"

He just shook his head. "There is no me and Billy Jo. Why does everyone keep insisting there's something between us when there isn't? We're friends, that's all. Actually, we're more like work buddies. I help her out with a problem and vice versa. We occasionally have coffee. We're friends, that's it, nothing more." He actually gestured, cutting his hand through the air.

"Uh-huh. You know, Mark, you may keep telling yourself that, but that doesn't mean it's true. I saw it the first time I met the girl, and I see it every time I see you two together. You know how some couples work and some don't."

He couldn't believe she was still talking about it. He just jabbed his finger at her, at a loss for words.

She put her mug down and lifted her hands. "Just saying, Mark, it wouldn't be a terrible thing."

Then the station door opened, and the chief walked in, and Gail started packing up. Great, a change of guards. The conversation about Billy Jo was over. Yet Mark was still stuck on the fact that it seemed everyone was talking about him and Billy Jo when there was nothing between them.

Chapter 20

She didn't think Carmen wore anything other than a deputy uniform, but there she was in a pair of blue jeans and a baby blue sweater. Her hair was tied back as it always was, though. She was slender, not curvy.

"You sure I can't get you a drink?" Billy Jo said. "Wine or beer? I picked some up because that's what Mark likes."

Carmen just waved her hand in response and pulled out a stool to sit at the island. "I don't drink," she said. "Water works for me."

Billy Jo filled a glass and slid it across the island in front of her, then lifted her own glass of red and took a swallow. "So I made a shepherd's pie because it's fast and easy. Hope that's okay, because I'm not making anything else."

Carmen only shrugged.

Billy Jo could see how uncomfortable she was, well aware that Mark still wasn't there. "So I presume Mark is on his way?" she said.

Carmen was staring at her with those dark eyes of hers, and she could see the minute the woman had taken her question the wrong way. "I would think so. He said he was coming over. He also told me to give you the benefit of the doubt, said you'd likely have some under-standing of my situation, as if you've lived through worse. He didn't elaborate, but I have to wonder what he meant. You know, you two dance around each other, pretending you're not involved, but you behave more like a couple than any I've ever seen. You know too much about each other. It was like he was trying to smooth over the fact that you stepped into my personal business, which no one ever does."

She paused before taking a swallow of her wine and resting the glass on the counter. So Mark had defended her. The thought should've made her happy. "You're still angry about what I said. I guess I could have never brought it up. That would probably have been the best option, right? We could both pretend we don't know anything and continue ignoring each other. You said Mark told you I understand your situation because I've lived through worse. Did he really say that? He didn't share anything?"

Carmen lifted her brow. She was messing with her. "No, apparently, he doesn't share our personal stories. Whatever he knows about you, he didn't tell me. Am I curious? Of course, but it's your business, not mine." She pulled her arms over her chest as she sat straighter on the stool, the awkward guest.

"He's right, though," Billy Jo said. "I know well how fucked up the system is. You said your sister has your kid. So you haven't seen him, then?"

Carmen only shook her head. "No. He's no longer mine."

She wondered what that meant. "You've given up your rights to him?"

"So you didn't go poking around in my file?" Carmen said. "I'm sure it's there, everything. It happened on this very island."

She heard a vehicle, Mark's Jeep. She should've been relieved, but instead she felt nervous in a way she couldn't remember ever feeling before. She wondered if that was why Carmen was watching her so intently.

"As you said, it's your business, not mine," Billy Jo said. "I told you before that I know only what I heard you say to Mark. I could have looked, and I suppose anyone else would have, but I had already heard enough. I imagine it would've been a hundred times worse, living it. I have my own past that isn't anyone's business, so I'm not about to start sticking my nose in yours. I only offered. You don't have to take me up on it. I invited you over to dinner because you remind me too much of myself. Being alone isn't always easy."

She heard the Jeep door close and knew it would be only seconds before Mark was in her place, and maybe that was why she could feel her heartbeat kicking up.

"My sister and I were taken from our mother when we were kids, pulled from the reservation," Carmen said. "My mother was taken from her parents, too, and she was never able to be a parent after living in the place they sent her—the place she was taken to have the Indian removed from her. What happened to her…some just never recover from it. She didn't. You know what I remember of her? Nothing. Drunkenness, empty bottles, and starving.

"I didn't even know I had a sister until I was trying to get my Native rights, and then I found her. She was adopted to a nice white family, as she said. I wasn't as lucky. So when everything came down on me the way it did, I knew I wasn't going to get a fair shake.

"I couldn't afford to pay for the kind of lawyer who'd have been able to make a difference and straighten out the perceptions of the people I was dealing with. My sister took my son, and it was conditional. I had to sign over my rights to him and stay away. She and her husband adopted him, and I promised never to call again. So no, you can't help me. No one can."

She heard the stairs creak, then a knock on the door. "Come in," she called out without pulling her gaze from Carmen, knowing Mark wouldn't have known any of what she'd just said.

The door opened, and he stepped inside.

"I picked up wine," he said. "Dinner smells good." He was dressed the way he always was, in that ratty jean jacket. She could hear his cowboy boots on the floor as he strode in.

"Thanks for the wine," she said, then gestured toward the fridge. "I picked you up some beer. It's in there."

He rested a really nice bottle of red, which happened to be one of her favorites, on the island before pulling open the fridge behind her and reaching for a beer. Carmen's brows lifted.

"So I made some calls for you about that little girl," he said, "and I spoke with Brice. He's out now."

Billy Jo turned as he leaned on the island not far

from her and popped the top of his beer can. "Oh. And…?"

Carmen dragged her gaze between the two of them, and she didn't want to analyze that too closely.

"He's moving back here—to his house, as he put it, the one Nia stole from him. With the charges against her, Dylan, and Harry and Beth, it seems everything will eventually work through the courts. He'll likely receive a settlement from the state for being wrongly convicted. He's angry, has every right to be, and said he's planning on taking Gabriele. He has some hoops to jump through still with the state. I guess once they have a kid in the system, it's never a matter of just turning her back over. But that's your department."

She realized he had done everything she'd asked and then some. "Thanks for digging," she said.

He only lifted his beer and took a swallow.

Carmen was looking at him before dragging her gaze over to her, a pointed look that only added to her unease. "You know what?" she said. "I'm going to leave you two to have dinner. I have things to do." Then she slid off the stool and took them in, and Billy Jo was positive an odd smile touched her lips.

"You're bailing?" Mark called out as Carmen started walking to the door, simply lifting her hand.

Billy Jo started after her in her slippers. She hadn't worn these blue jeans in a long time, and even the comfortable red shirt she wore was a little on the dressier side than normal. "You know, dinner is almost ready," she said, "and I invited you for dinner."

Carmen pulled on her light fleece jacket. Mark was still in the kitchen, and Carmen looked past her to him and shook her head. "Being a third wheel isn't my thing," she said. "This thing between you two, the thing you both keep denying, you can tell yourself it's nothing, but we all see it. So enjoy your dinner together, and since we're not sticking our noses into each other's business, you should know that Mark may want everyone to believe he's not such a great guy, but that's why he is one. Then there's the way he looks at you." Her gaze was imploring for a moment.

Billy Jo had to remind herself to breathe.

Carmen opened the door and glanced past her. "Goodnight, Mark," she called out, then walked out the door.

Billy Jo closed it and turned to see Mark pulling open her oven and lifting out the casserole dish, making himself at home. She strode back over to the island, where he was resting the dish on potholders.

"So what was that really about, her leaving?" he said. He was perceptive, too.

"Oh, I think Carmen needs smaller steps. Maybe next time she'll make it through dinner. So are you going to dish up, too?"

He let his gaze linger, and she took in the wine he had brought over. He pulled open the cupboard and reached for two plates. "Well, tell me about your day," he said as he reached for a large serving spoon. When she laughed softly, he glanced back to her and said, "You should do that more often." He gestured with the spoon toward her.

"Well, look at us, sitting here, about to have some simple comfort food and converse like normal people."

"Ah, but that's the thing, Billy Jo. We're anything but normal." He slid her plate on the island and dished up another for himself, and she took in his back.

She didn't want to like this man, but she could feel her heartbeat kicking up as he backed over, holding his plate and two forks. She reached for one and took in the way he was looking at her, feeling that fear but doing it anyway.

"Mark, just promise me one thing."

He rested his plate across from her on the island and went to dig in as he looked over to her. "Sure, what is it?"

She jabbed her fork into the casserole and considered it for only a second. Then she nodded. "That no matter what, we'll always be friends first."

He said nothing for a second, then nodded as well. "Yeah, I can do that."

Turn the page for a sneak peek of
*THE TRAP the next book in the BILLY JO MCCABE
MYSTERY*
Available in print, eBook & audio

The Trap
BILLY JO MCCABE MYSTERY

On a cold and rainy night, Billy Jo McCabe receives a troubling phone call about a child in trouble. But when she shows up alone, things quickly go sideways, and she realizes her mistake.

In her role as a social worker, Billy Jo rarely expects to walk into trouble, and the last thing she ever wants to do is call for backup from arrogant redheaded detective

Mark Friessen, whom she's beginning to depend on in the kinds of ways she shouldn't. When she gets a call late one night about a child in trouble, Billy Jo doesn't hesitate to drive out alone. However, she arrives to find the property abandoned, and with only one bar of battery on her phone and no cell service, she realizes far too late that she's walked into a dark situation.

When Billy Jo doesn't show up for work the next day, Detective Friessen is called in to find her. As he follows her trail and retraces her steps, he soon discovers her car abandoned in a field, and he has an uneasy feeling that her disappearance isn't an accident. The more he searches, the more he fears that this is a trap—not for her but for him.

The Trap
CHAPTER 1

What was that sound?

The ringing came from a distance as Billy Jo stared at the arrogant redhead. He seemed to look right through her…

When she jolted awake, she realized it was her phone ringing from somewhere in the apartment.

Mark Friessen had been in her dreams.

She tossed back the covers, and her bare feet hit the icy floor in the pitch black. She flicked on her bedside light and hurried out of the bedroom. Her cell phone was on the island in the kitchen, and the screen was lit up when she landed on it.

"Hello?" she said, then cleared her throat, still feeling the cobwebs of sleep and her anger at how Mark had looked at her. The red digital clock on the stove read 1:10 a.m.

"Ms. McCabe, this is the program director from DCFS. I'm filling in for Grant. I apologize for calling at this late hour, but we have an emergency."

She didn't recognize the voice. What had he said his name was?

"I'm sorry, who is this?" she said, shivering as she strode back to her bedroom, where Harley was curled up asleep on the bed, half under the covers she'd tossed back. He didn't stir.

"Lane Fuller," the man said. "Again, I apologize for the late hour, but a report has come in about a child in trouble. I need you to immediately pick up the child and arrange for emergency placement."

Her hand went to her head, and she brushed back her hair, which she knew was sticking up everywhere. She grabbed her ratty plush gray housecoat and shrugged one arm in as she hurried back into the kitchen, then flicked on the bright overhead light. She blinked, her heart thudding with the familiar warning that came at her every time she woke in the night.

"What happened?" she said. She spotted her bag and juggled the phone between her shoulder and her ear as she pulled out the pen and notebook she always kept tucked inside. She instinctively rolled her shoulders, feeling the chill of the night.

"Not sure on the details. All I know is we're to pick up the kid. The name here is…" The sound he made was cold and unfeeling, and she couldn't shake the suspicion that he possessed the familiar trait of too many in this business. She'd become accustomed to the desensitization, just something it seemed came with this job. Otherwise, it could eat people up. She, though, still saw the eyes of all the children, the hope that dimmed there, every night before she slept.

Maybe that was why she felt haunted now.

"Ah, here it is," he said. "Whitney Chandler, and

here's the address." He rattled it off, and she scribbled it down, wondering whether this job ever got easier.

"And how old is the child? Did something happen? The parents…?"

"I told you this is all I have. It's just an emergency placement. Go get her, find a bed for her tonight, and you can iron out all the details in the morning," he said. Then he hung up, and Billy Jo just stared at the disconnected phone, glancing at the time again and wondering why it seemed emergencies happened only in the middle of the night.

She hated this. Worse, she hadn't even met the child but could already feel her anguish.

She pulled on thick socks and opted for sweats and a sweatshirt, then ran a brush over her hair, hearing the rain pattering on the roof. She reached for her heavy warm raincoat and shoved her feet into her lined rainboots, then quickly searched up the address. It was a part of the island that she knew was rural and dark.

Great, just perfect for a late-night visit!

"Seriously, why does the bad kind of shit have to happen after dark?" she muttered, pissed off. There was something about the night that always had her on edge.

Billy Jo reached for her phone, seeing Mark's name in her contacts, and could feel the unease. *It was just a dream,* she reminded herself as she thumbed past his name. She opened Pam's contact and dialed, then put it on speaker and listened to it ring once, twice. Then it went to voicemail.

"Ah, dammit… Pam, it's Billy Jo. I need you to get up. I got a call from some guy filling in for Grant, and I'm doing an emergency placement. There's a kid in trouble. Not sure of any of the details, but I need you to find me a bed for her tonight…" She heard the beep and knew she'd just been cut off.

She reached for her bag and then opened the drawer in the kitchen island to pull out a flashlight to tuck into it. As she strode to the door, the phone to her ear, dialing Pam again, she held the notebook open to the address.

"What!"

At least this time she answered.

"This is Billy Jo. I just left you a message. Sorry to call in the middle of the night." She pulled open the door and flicked on the outside light. The rain was heavy, pounding down, making everything impossible— seeing, driving, just being out in it. "I just got a call from the program supervisor. I think he said his name was Lane. I have to pick up a kid in trouble."

She rattled off the address and then tucked the notebook in her coat pocket as she stood in the open doorway, her hood up. Then she stepped out and pulled the door closed, the rain pelting down on her. "Look, I'm driving out there now, so find me a bed if you can. Call me back and let me know where to take her."

The way Pam sighed on the other end summed up exactly what she was feeling. "I'll see what I can find. Why is it that it seems these calls happen only in the middle of the night?"

Hadn't she just thought the same thing? She didn't answer, remembering her nights in foster care, lying there in the dark. That was when everything bad could and would happen.

"Oh, and Pam, whatever place you find, try to make sure I won't have to worry that I'm pulling this kid from one bad situation and sticking her in another."

"I'll do my best," was all she said.

Billy Jo hung up and tucked the phone in her bag, then made her way down the steps, the rain making everything difficult. She splashed through the puddles to her new Nissan and yanked open the door, then tossed her bag in across to the passenger side and climbed in.

She should have brought a towel, as the water dripped off her. She stared at the outside light and started her car, letting it warm for a second before flicking on the heat and pulling down the darkened driveway to the road.

The wipers were on high, whirring back and forth so fast as she gripped the steering wheel, trying to see, but the rain came down so hard that they couldn't clear it fast enough. Worse, the fog had settled in, and she white-knuckled the steering wheel.

"Damn, I hate nights like this," she said as she struggled to see, searching for the faded white lines on the road as she rounded a bend. The road was treelined on both sides now, and she slowed as the water splashed under her wheels. She turned right and had to flick on her high-beams, seeing darkened driveways, some with numbers, some without.

"114, where are you?" she said over and over, slowing to a crawl, seeing trees and driveways, only two with numbers by the road. "Sometimes I really hate this island."

She slammed on the brakes when she spotted a small sign with an address in white letters, realizing she'd gone too far. She pulled out her notebook and flipped to the page with the address, remembering the directions she'd pulled up, feeling uneasy because of the night and the quiet.

With her foot on the brake, the car idling, she

reached for her phone in her bag and saw that it had only one bar of battery left. How had she managed not to charge it when it had been plugged in and supposedly charging in the kitchen? Or had it?

"Stupid, stupid, Billy Jo." She made a rude noise and tapped the phone to her forehead. Her frustration only added to the unease in her stomach, that sick feeling she didn't think was ever far away. "Come on, keep it together," she muttered as she rummaged through her purse for her charger, which wasn't there. "Shit! Idiot!"

She slapped the steering wheel, then forced herself to pull in a breath and put her car in reverse. She flicked on the rear wipers and backed up until she stopped at a rutted treelined driveway she was positive had to belong to the house she was looking for. She flicked off her high-beams when the fog had her seeing a sea of white —and then she saw it, a darkened house with what looked to be an older pickup parked out front.

She squeezed the steering wheel with both hands and pulled up beside the truck, then took in the house, a small two-story. She thought she saw a light on upstairs. At the same time, she'd expected someone to be there already.

The police? That would be Mark, who she again reminded herself was both arrogant and unhealthy for her wellbeing. The dream had been a reminder that she was depending on him in ways that would end up breaking her.

She turned off her car and picked up her phone, but when she went to call Pam again, the phone flashed from one bar to no service. She lifted it and moved it until she saw the bar again, then pulled up Mark's number and wrote a quick text: *Got a call to pick up a kid in trouble. Wondering if you received anything? Here now, but no one else is...*

Her thumb hovered over the send button. She wanted to kick herself for doing exactly what she shouldn't be. "Nope, nope, not happening," she said as she deleted the message. The battery was now in the red.

"This is just great, Billy Jo," she said under her breath. "Pam can't even call you now to let you know where to take the kid, and where are you but in between crazytown and creepyville?"

She opened her door and gave it a shove, then reached for the flashlight in her purse. She stepped out right into a puddle, the rain still pouring down. She closed the door and flicked on the flashlight, her breath fogging as she started past the truck to the three wide steps up to the front door. Solid wood and no doorbell.

Her hand was wet and cold. She fisted it to knock, feeling the hair rise on the back of her neck and that same sick feeling she'd had as a kid, when everything had always gone from bad to worse. It was the strange doors she remembered so vividly: old, worn, dirty, marked up or scraped and patched. Strange doors leading to strange people and houses, and a feeling of desperation and anger that never went away.

Billy Jo forced herself to knock on the wooden door and took another second to see where she was. There was no one around. Rain was the only sound she heard as she pictured her uncharged cell phone in the car. Then she knocked again, and this time she knew someone was on the other side of the door. It was just a feeling.

"Hello? Can you open the door, please? My name is Billy Jo McCabe, with DCFS. We got a call about…"

She heard the click of the door being unlocked, then the squeak as it opened. She was suddenly aware of a faint light on the other side—then a clang of metal. She focused everything on that sound of a gun being cocked, a sound she knew too well. She stared in horror, seeing everything and nothing as she reminded herself to breathe.

Someone with a raspy voice said, "Well, then I guess you'd better come in."

At the icy chill that ricocheted straight down through her, she realized her mistake. She was there alone, with no backup, no help. As she stared at the steel of the gun and the pale hand holding it, she knew that whatever this was, she was in over her head.

About the Author

"Lorhainne Eckhart is one of my go to authors when I want a guaranteed good book. So many twists and turns, but also so much love and such a strong sense of family."

(Lora W., Reviewer)

New York Times & USA Today bestseller Lorhainne Eckhart is best known for her writing Raw Relatable Real Romances, where "Morals and family are running themes. Danger, romance, and a drive to do what is right will see you glued to the page." As one fan calls her, she is the "Queen of the family saga." (aherman) writing "the ups and downs of what goes on within a family but also with some suspense, angst and of course a bit of romance thrown in for good measure." Follow Lorhainne on Bookbub to receive alerts on New Releases and Sales and join her mailing list at LorhainneEckhart.com for her Monday Blog, books news, giveaways and FREE reads. With over 120 books, audiobooks, and multiple series published and available at all retailers now translated into six languages. She is a multiple recipient of the Readers' Favorite Award for Suspense and Romance, and lives in the Pacific Northwest on an island, is the mother of three, her oldest has autism and she is an advocate for never giving up on your dreams.

"Lorhainne Eckhart has this uncanny way of just hitting the spot every time with her books."

(Caroline L., Reviewer)

The O'Connells: *The O'Connells of Livingston, Montana are not your typical family. A riveting collection of stories surrounding the ups and downs of what goes on within a family but also with some suspense, angst and of course a bit of romance thrown in for good measure "I thought I loved the Friessens, but I absolutely adore the O'Connell's. Each and every book has totally different genres of stories but the one thing in common is how she is able to wrap it around the family which is the heart of each story." (C. Logue)*

The Friessens: *An emotional big family romance series, the Friessen family siblings find their relationships tested, lay their hearts on the line, and discover lasting love! "Lorhainne Eckhart is one of my go to authors when I want a guaranteed good book. So many twists and turns, but also so much love and such a strong sense of family." (Lora W., Reviewer)*

The Parker Sisters: *The Parker Sisters are a close-knit family, and like any other family they have their ups and downs. "Eckhart has crafted another intense family drama…The character development is outstanding, and the emotional investment is high…" (Aherman, Reviewer)*

The McCabe Brothers: *Join the five McCabe siblings on their journeys to the dark and dangerous side of love! An intense, exhilarating collection of romantic thrillers you won't want to miss. — "Eckhart has a new series that is definitely worth the read. The queen of the family saga started this series with a spin-off of her wildly successful Friessen series." From a Readers' Favorite award—winning author and "queen of the family saga" (Aherman)*

Billy Jo McCabe Mystery: *The social worker and the cop, an unlikely couple drawn together on a small, secluded Pacific Northwest island where nothing is as it seems. Protecting the innocent comes at a cost, and what seems to be a sleepy, quiet town is anything but.*

Lorhainne loves to hear from her readers! You can connect with me at:
www.LorhainneEckhart.com
lorhainneeckhart.le@gmail.com

facebook.com/AuthorLorhainneEckhart

twitter.com/LEckhart

instagram.com/lorhainneeckhart

bookbub.com/profile/lorhainne-eckhart

pinterest.com/lorhainneeckhart

Also by Lorhainne Eckhart

The Outsider Series
The Forgotten Child (Brad and Emily)
A Baby and a Wedding *(An Outsider Series Short)*
Fallen Hero (Andy, Jed, and Diana)
The Search *(An Outsider Series Short)*
The Awakening (Andy and Laura)
Secrets (Jed and Diana)
Runaway (Andy and Laura)
Overdue *(An Outsider Series Short)*
The Unexpected Storm (Neil and Candy)
The Wedding (Neil and Candy)

The Friessens: A New Beginning
The Deadline (Andy and Laura)
The Price to Love (Neil and Candy)
A Different Kind of Love (Brad and Emily)
A Vow of Love, A Friessen Family Christmas

The Friessens
The Reunion
The Bloodline (Andy & Laura)
The Promise (Diana & Jed)
The Business Plan (Neil & Candy)
The Decision (Brad & Emily)
First Love (Katy)
Family First
Leave the Light On
In the Moment

In the Family
In the Silence
In the Charm
Unexpected Consequences
It Was Always You
The First Time I Saw You
Welcome to My Arms
Welcome to Boston
I'll Always Love You
Ground Rules
A Reason to Breathe
You Are My Everything
Anything For You
The Homecoming
Stay Away From My Daughter
The Bad Boy
A Place of Our Own
The Visitor
All About Devon
Long Past Dawn
How to Heal a Heart
Keep Me In Your Heart

The O'Connells
The Neighbor
The Third Call
The Secret Husband
The Quiet Day
The Commitment
The Missing Father
The Hometown Hero
Justice
The Family Secret

The Fallen O'Connell
The Return of the O'Connells
And The She Was Gone
The Stalker
The O'Connell Family Christmas
The Girl Next Door

The McCabe Brothers
Don't Stop Me (Vic)
Don't Catch Me (Chase)
Don't Run From Me (Aaron)
Don't Hide From Me (Luc)
Don't Leave Me (Claudia)
Out of Time

A Billy Jo McCabe Mystery
Nothing As it Seems
Hiding in Plain Sight
The Cold Case
The Trap
Above the Law

The Wilde Brothers
The One (Joe and Margaret)
The Honeymoon, A Wilde Brothers Short
Friendly Fire (Logan and Julia)
Not Quite Married, A Wilde Brothers Short
A Matter of Trust (Ben and Carrie)
The Reckoning, A Wilde Brothers Christmas
Traded (Jake)
Unforgiven (Samuel)
The Holiday Bride

Married in Montana
His Promise
Love's Promise
A Promise of Forever

The Parker Sisters
Thrill of the Chase
The Dating Game
Play Hard to Get
What We Can't Have
Go Your Own Way
A June Wedding

Kate & Walker
One Night
Edge of Night
Last Night

Walk the Right Road Series
The Choice
Lost and Found
Merkaba
Bounty
Blown Away: The Final Chapter

The Saved Series
Saved
Vanished
Captured

Single Titles
He Came Back
Loving Christine

For my German Readers
Die Außenseiter-Reihe
Der Vergessene Junge
Der Gefallene Held

For my French Readers
L'ENFANT OUBLIÉ